THE RUNAWAY WIFE

JANE BONANDER

To my patient loving husband, Richard Noer

PROLOGUE

Lake Forest, Illinois–March 1882

*E*rnest Jarvis was dying. He knew it, his doctor knew it, his family knew it, but he was the only one who knew he would die tonight. His fingers, once long and strong, were now weak and trembling as he folded the missive in half and then again to make it small enough to hide between the pages of the book.

She read to him every night; surely she would find it. He would be gone by morning. He would miss the sound of her voice as she read, for she enjoyed the words perhaps even more than he did. Truthfully, the story, *Little Women*, was her choice. He had acquiesced, as he always did with her.

But she would heed the letter. She was his daughter through and through. She would not believe his words were merely the fears of an old man on the verge of death. She had to know what he discovered before it was too late.

CHAPTER 1

March, 1883—One year after her father's death

*A*nastasia heard her husband on the stairs and immediately felt sick to her stomach. She gripped her silver handled brush and appeared calm as she continued to run it through her hair, but, as usual, her insides were in turmoil.

Oliver stepped into the room; she avoided his gaze and kept hers on the top of her dressing table where a half dozen bottles of expensive perfumes and lotions were carefully placed on one side, an inch and a quarter apart. On the other side was her Moroccan leather jewelry case, full to the brim with things she rarely if ever wore. Everything inside was neatly partitioned off. *We don't like messes, do we, dahling?* She clenched her teeth. His British accent no longer appealed to her.

He came toward her and placed his hands on her shoulders, dipping one down into her dressing gown, over her breast. Her nipple automatically tightened, but not from desire.

"Ah, I can still arouse you, can't I?" He gave the breast a squeeze, then squeezed it a little harder, causing her to swallow a gasp.

She clenched her jaw and squelched a shiver of revulsion and glanced in the mirror. He wore his gray flannel suit with a gray and red striped cravat. His dark hair, silver at the temples, was immaculately combed, and she smelled his expensive pomade. Had she not loathed him she might have found him handsome. She did at one time. His diamond and sapphire ring sparkled on his little finger. The ring she purchased for him when they wed. With her money, which of course, was now his to spend as well.

"Good morning, *ma Cherie*." Once a long time ago, or so it seemed, his words had softened her. Ugh. Now when he spoke French she wanted to retch. She had preened when he called her 'my dear.' No more. When you are called *dear* in one breath and *cow* in the next, it's hard to feel special.

"I've ordered a bath for you this morning. To soothe what hurts you."

How very thoughtful since you are the one who left the bruises. But she knew the routine.

Her gaze returned to the top of the dressing table. "Thank you," she answered, forcing a smile.

He drew a chair up beside her and gently touched the bruise on her chin. She flinched and pulled away. "You know, Anastasia, if you wouldn't embarrass me in public, these things wouldn't happen."

They had dined with one of the company's biggest clients the night before. Ernest Jarvis had amassed a great fortune in mining in California years ago. After Anastasia's father died, her Uncle Horace led the business and had given Oliver a fine position when he married Anastasia.

Of course, there had been those months before the wedding when he wooed her, appeared to really care for her and made every effort to become part of the family. He had come to them with a proper introduction from an old family friend in London who had, unfortunately, died. He was mannerly and presented a confident front, something that had appealed to Horace after Papa died.

Anastasia had since learned that her husband could be anyone he chose to be. To everyone else, he was charming, his personality magnetic. To her, if they were alone, he was critical of everything she did, constantly trying to make her into something she definitely was not. And he was mean, cruel, and brutish.

Had he thought marrying into Chicago's society would yield him a proper debutante, he was mightily disappointed for Anastasia was not. It had not taken her long to realize that his interest in her was merely financial.

Earlier yesterday, Anastasia had spent hours in her garden, working so intensely that she hadn't realized how exhausted she had become. At the restaurant where they dined with the client and his wife, Anastasia tried to stifle a yawn but didn't catch it in time. That was all it took. She knew what would happen once they got home. And the punishment never failed to fit the crime in Oliver's eyes. He had slapped her so hard she fell backwards into the corner of a table. She didn't think it had broken the skin, and the bruise on her cheek was minor. But the contusion on her back was large and sore.

Sex always followed the beatings. She had long since stopped calling it love making as there was no love or interest involved on her part. But as long as she lay there and didn't resist, he seemed satisfied. She learned early on that if she fought him, he hurt her more. He enjoyed inflicting pain.

"Remember, cocktails with the Smiths at seven. And do not wear that awful purple frock you seem to enjoy so much. It gives your skin a ghastly hue." He gave her a gentle kiss on the forehead. Before he left, he added, "And I was told you gardened yesterday. Do not do anything strenuous today. I won't have you yawning in front of our guests—again."

She finally heard him taking the stairs to the floor below and wiped away the kiss on her forehead. Her life was full of 'do nots'. As it happened, she had planned to wear the purple gown because it was elegant and comfortable. To wear it now would only give him fuel for the fire.

As she went into her bath, she heard him say something to the butler before he left the house. When she heard the door slam, she shrugged out of her silk robe and lowered herself into the tub of bubbly, warm water, wondering yet again how long she could take his abuse. She lifted the sponge from the side of the tub and scrubbed at her breast, hoping to wipe away all of his touch.

She had no allies in this war; even her mother refused to believe it wasn't her fault. "Just stop doing what it is that gets him angry," she suggested. *Well, thank you, Mother dearest, for the support.* Her sister, Sarah, or Sally as Anastasia called her, much to her mother's dismay, would be on her side if she knew what Oliver was doing to her, but Anastasia had resisted the urge to confide in her, for it would only upset her. There was nothing she could do about it anyway as she lived in Atlanta with her husband, Jacob, and their two daughters. Anastasia rarely saw them, and she missed them all terribly.

She often wondered if motherhood was in the cards for her. Would Oliver react differently toward her if she were to carry his child? Would he feel the same pride that most fathers-to-be feel? Or would he still batter her around despite her condition.

It had been a year since her papa died, and her grief had softened, but it would never go away. The sore had scabbed over, but she still felt the loss. And her mother, who wore her widow's weeds until just recently, often lamented being widowed. Anastasia didn't know what the relationship had been like between her parents, but she could tell that her mother suffered too. Although Grace Jarvis wasn't a terribly introspective person and rarely took anyone into her confidence, Anastasia often saw sadness in her eyes. It was at those times she wished they were close; her mother never shared feelings with her. Just criticism.

Papa had been her champion, probably because Anastasia had so many of his qualities—bad ones, her mother admonished. But it was he who taught her to ride and shoot and hunt and swim, much to her mother's disappointment.

"Young ladies of your social standing should be learning the skills I learned when I was your age," her mother rebuked. "Your needlepoint is atrocious. You're incapable of pouring a correct cup of tea, and you pay far too much attention to the help. They aren't your friends, Anastasia. They're paid to be here. And when you take a seat, you should cross your legs at the ankles. You often plop yourself down like a washer woman."

Before her marriage, all Anastasia had to do was walk into a room, and her mother would look up at her and say, "You're too tall. Can't you hunch a bit? No man is going to ask for your hand if you're bigger and taller than he is."

Yes, she was tall, and yes, she was fit in ways other women frowned upon. But her love of swimming had given her a toned body, not one of fat.

On any given humid summer day in Chicago, her mother would complain, "Your hair is absolutely unruly. You look like a gypsy." Really, Anastasia thought, a gypsy? Her mother, pampered and sheltered all her life, had probably never even seen a gypsy. And if she had, she probably would have run away screaming. Or fainted, although the Jarvis women never fainted.

If Anastasia found something amusing, her mother would chide, "You laugh like a longshoreman just like your father did. I don't know of any young woman who eats as much as you do. One day you'll be sorry when your backside gets as big as a donkey's. You have all of your father's traits right down to the cleft in your chin. You should have been a boy."

Perhaps it was a back-handed compliment, but occasionally her mother would add, "It's not enough to have nice skin and a pretty face."

Yes, she was tall. She and Oliver looked eye to eye when they stood, and Anastasia never wore shoes with heels. In fact, she'd stopped wearing any heels long ago. And Oliver was no help, really. Whether it was vanity or the need to control, the fact that she was tall did bother him. He often made her sit just to mask the fact that they looked eye to eye. She wondered why he married her in the first place. Ah, yes, she remembered with a twist of her mouth, her money. And apparently, he was in need of a punching bag.

And yes, her laugh was robust. Like her Papa's. Or at least it used to be. Not much to laugh about now days was there?

Her gaze caught her reflection in the mirror at the end of the tub. Was she pretty? She didn't think so. She often thought her mother just said that to make up for all the negative qualities she rattled off in front of her. Her hair was nearly black, and the curls were hard to tame. She secretly plucked her eyebrows so there wouldn't be just one long one crawling over her eyes. Her blue eyes were nice, she supposed, but everyone she knew had blue eyes, so they weren't special. Normal nose, normal mouth, lips a little fuller than usual, but she really looked quite average.

Sally was the pretty one—the complete opposite of her. Petite, feminine, glossy light honey brown hair that had a wave in it. She looked very much like their mother, although, Anastasia thought, she was a better person. Again, not a nice thing to say about one's mother, but there it was. And although she pretended her mother's actions toward her didn't affect her, they did. No one wants to always be at odds with one's mother.

She lathered her sponge with rose soap, dipped it into the water, and squeezed it over her shoulders, feeling it run down her back, over the most recent welt. In a few minutes her maid, Clarice, whom she trusted like a friend, would be in to help her, not that she wanted or needed help, but if word got to Oliver than she had told her maid not to bother, there would be hell to pay for both of them. Clarice wouldn't say anything to anyone, but surely one of the other maids would.

Closing her eyes, she settled back against the tub, resting lightly against her bruise. She needed a plan. As much as she wanted out of her marriage, she knew she must take her time. And once a plan was in place, she had to be very certain that her husband wouldn't think to follow her. She couldn't merely run off. He'd be after her in a flash. There was so much to consider. What to take with her, how to smuggle it off the estate. Whom to trust—if anyone. Where to go…that would take some thinking.

In the next month or so, there were some social functions she couldn't avoid. And she didn't think the venues were right for an escape. And she would need money. Of course, she had her own, but Oliver paid careful attention to what she spent. Withdrawing a large sum would be unwise. She had some available to her but certainly not enough to begin a new life. Oliver controlled everything. Everything. From the beginning her mother had thought it was for the best, because after all, Anastasia wasn't your typical socialite. In her mother's eyes, she was unable to run a household. God, how many times had she heard that?

She didn't have a husband. She had a jailer. A warden. A keeper.

The door to the bath opened. "Are you ready for me, ma'am?"

Anastasia brushed a stray curl away from her face. "Yes, Clarice. Let's get it over with."

Clarice entered and closed the door behind her. "Mr. Oliver left you a gift on your breakfast tray. But I don't think you're going to like what he wants you to eat for breakfast." She took the sponge from Anastasia and when she saw the contusion on her back, she gasped. "Oh, he did this last night?" She sucked in a breath as she studied it. "He broke the skin this time. I'll put something over it to keep it dry."

Clarice was the only one who saw what Oliver did to her. Time and again she witnessed the bruises, the bumps, even the shiner he had given her one night after he felt she'd had too much sherry. She relaxed as Clarice gently washed her back, going so lightly over her contusion she hardly felt it. Yes, she thought. Beat her up and buy her off.

Whatever he bought her she didn't need or want. She glanced at Clarice. She was a pretty young thing with hair the color of sunshine and a peachy glow to her skin. And she was innocent and loyal. How pleasant it would be to have her as a traveling companion, but it would be a dead giveaway if both of them disappeared at the same time.

"So my hotcakes and bacon order didn't make it to the kitchen?" Her voice dripped with sarcasm.

"No, ma'am. I'm afraid it's dry toast and a fruit plate."

The night before, when they were at dinner, she had ordered a piece of cheesecake after the meal. He had looked at her sharply but hadn't said anything. She paid for it when they got home. That plus the yawn had put Oliver in a particularly foul mood.

"Really?" he had snarled. "Cheesecake? My God, Anastasia, you keep eating like that and you will become repugnant to me."

It was funny, she thought. She was repugnant to him now.

"I could bring you something else." Clarice's voice was sympathetic.

"Thank you, Clarice, but the toast and fruit will be fine. There is coffee, isn't there?" That was probably the only thing Oliver didn't think would make her fat.

"Yes."

"Make sure I get plenty of cream and sugar, will you please? The more the better."

Clarice laughed softly. "Of course. What about the gift?"

"Just put it with the others in my jewelry box, Clarice."

"Don't you want to know what it is?"

Anastasia stood and climbed from the tub. "I suppose I'd better know so I can thank him properly."

Clarice took Anastasia's robe off the hook and helped her into it. "I know it's not my place, but I can't help thinking you should tell someone what he does to you."

Anastasia tied the belt around her waist. "I told my mother, and she basically told me to stop doing what angers him."

With a sympathetic smile, Clarice left the bath and returned with the gift. Anastasia opened the ornate box and nestled inside was a bangle bracelet with fancy lapped ends. It looked like a coiled snake. How appropriate, she thought, snapping the top shut. That's what he was doing to her, squeezing the life out of her.

May—1883

The day of reckoning had come, and she was ready. Anastasia had missed the launch that was to take them to the yacht. Purposefully, of course. Oliver was irate and had gone on without her. Now, as she approached the small dingy that was tied to the dock, she stopped and took one last look back at her home.

It was beautiful, tall and majestic, brilliantly white in the sunshine. Porch pillars made it look quite southern, like so many of the homes she'd seen in Atlanta where Sally lived. There were immaculate flower beds bursting with pinks and yellows that reminded Anastasia of sheets of velvet. Lawn shrubs trimmed, smooth, and round. And grass meticulously cared for and so green it looked like carpeting.

Her gaze went to the big oak tree on the edge of the property. The tree she climbed high into the branches so she could see the lake. Until the day she fell and broke her arm. She was not allowed to climb it ever again, although she did, when she knew no one was paying any attention to her, which was often enough.

A strong wave of nostalgia swept through her. She was actually leaving everything she had ever known, going into a world unfamiliar and strange to her.

As she stepped into the dingy, there was a flip in her stomach, a slight misstep in her stride, a hesitation in her determination. But there was no turning back.

CHAPTER 2

Willow River, California, Early June, 1883

(Just inland from Big Sur)
Journal Entry—Ravens and Crows:

Though they are very much alike, crows and ravens differ physically in many ways:
The crow's feathers are less shiny than the raven's, which are shiny with a wet sheen. The crow's bill is small and flat; the raven's bigger, powerful, and curved with a tuft of hair on the top.
The crow is smaller in size; the raven is almost the size of a red-tailed hawk—

The door to the sheriff's office burst open, slamming against the wall. "Sheriff! Sheriff! They're at it again! Come quick!" Young Davey Pine's face was squished into a frown, and he was sweating. His copper colored hair lay slicked down over his forehead. "They're going at it somfin' awful. I think Ma's gonna kill him this time."

Jesse Wolfe closed his journal where he recorded the flora and fauna of the area and the number of wildfires that cropped up over the past season. In the back he entered activities of seal and otter poachers. He tucked the journal into a drawer and unfolded his brawny frame from his chair. When he stood, he bumped his head on the lantern hanging from the ceiling over his desk. With a guttural curse he grabbed his hat off the peg by the door and followed Davey outside, keeping stride as the boy ran to his parents' cabin near the river.

A week rarely passed that Bert and Margot Pine didn't get into a fight. And it wasn't just a little squabble. One would likely kill the other if Jesse didn't intercede. Well, actually, Bert was more apt to take the beating, for he often ruffled Margot's feathers. During his eight years as sheriff Jesse had learned that men in this town had a way of pissing off their women, probably because of the active poker games held at the saloon.

The sight he came upon wasn't all that unusual. Bert and Margot were circling one another, Bert trying to worm his way out of his troubles and Margot wielding a cast iron skillet.

Jesse stepped in between them and wrestled the skillet from Margot's clenched fist. "What was it this time, Margot?"

Her paisley scarf was askew and part of the bun at the back of her neck had come loose. Her reddish blond hair hung to her shoulders. When she realized he was there, her face lit up. "Well, good morning, sheriff. How's that sweet daughter of yours?"

Bert added, his voice pleasant, "Seen your filly at the smithy yesta'day, sheriff. Hope it ain't serious."

Jesse didn't understand it. The moment he stepped into the room both of their attitudes changed.

Jesse studied the two, ignoring their pleasantries. Calm as cucumbers, both of them. He put the iron skillet on the table and planted his fists on his hips. "What's the fuss about this time?"

"It's him, of course," Margot accused, tossing her head in her husband's direction. "He didn't come home until it was time to milk the goat this morning."

Jesse glanced at Bert, who was studying the rag rug in front of the door. "Bert?"

Bert scrunched his face, making him look a bit like a dog

with a pushed-in muzzle. He shook his head. "Had me a poker hand last night that I didn't think no one could beat."

Jesse didn't need to hear the rest. Bert Pine was a fair poker player, but when he got ahead, he couldn't quite make himself quit. It was usually the reason Jesse was called to the cabin: Bert won a good hand and kept playing until his pockets were empty. Margot reared up and went at him with a skillet or an ax, and Davey ran for help.

Jesse glanced around the cabin. He could smell something delicious cooking on the stove. Margot was a good cook. And she kept a neat and tidy cabin. One would think that alone would keep Bert on the straight and narrow, but what could he do? Put them both in a cell for disturbing the peace? They lived far enough away from everyone else, so really, the only peace disturbed was Jesse's.

He turned toward the door. "Gracie Jane is fine, Margot, and my filly just needed a new shoe. Don't make Davey come for me again. Not this week, anyway." With that, he went outside and saw a familiar horse blanket folded up on a rickety rocker on the porch.

"Davey," he called.

The boy peeked out the door. "Sir?"

"Isn't that Chappy Miller's horse blanket?"

Davey looked a bit sheepish. "Dunno. I found it layin' by itself. Didn't see no one around. Figured it was left there."

Davey had a bit of a problem with taking other folks' things. "I think it belongs to Chappy. Maybe you should bring it to him."

Davey stared at the ground and gave Jesse a nod.

Jesse left, his long strides covering the dry, packed earth. Dust rose up in plumes; the rainy season was ahead of them. This time of year, the scrub oaks that grew in abundance outside of town took on a grayish hue, almost appearing like they were covered in dust. Even at the best of times they weren't a pretty tree.

He returned to the jail to check on his prisoner, Lester Johnson, who had drunk too much and hauled off and punched the bartender over at the saloon the night before. Jesse's deputy,

Lloyd, was Lester's brother. Lester was a troublemaker in the truest sense of the word. Not only was he a mean drunk, he often took to the shores along the coast to kill sea otter and sell the pelts. He killed them all right. He clubbed them to death. But so far, Jesse hadn't caught him at it.

Jesse went into the back room and stood before the cell. Lester glared up at him from the cot.

"You sober enough to go home?" Jesse asked.

Lester swung his legs over the edge and stood, stretching his back and releasing a loud belch. "Stayin' sober is no fun, Sheriff." He smiled as he said it, but Jesse saw the mean mischief behind his smile.

Jesse opened the cell door, and Lester followed him into the office, gave him a cocky salute, and left the jail.

Jesse stepped out and watched him swagger down the street toward the saloon, a tall, lean young man with a head full of dark, wavy hair, unlike his brother's, whose hair always looked like it had been struck by lightning. He wondered how brothers could be so different. Lloyd was honest, eager to help and learn, and trustworthy. Lester was anything but.

Once he had asked Lloyd how they could possibly be related, and the deputy's answer was, "Ma says Lester is the son of the devil. Which is strange, come to think of it, since me and Lester have the same pa."

Jesse turned the other way and walked to the boarding house for a cup of coffee. The owner, Ruta Ives, was a transplanted Scotswoman who had followed her husband from Scotland to California years before in search of gold. Needless to say, no gold was found, and her husband, Heck, took off, leaving Ruta to fend for herself.

An odd but enterprising woman, Ruta opened a much needed boarding house which continued to thrive in Willow River. And her coffee was strong and often laced with whiskey, to which Jesse added milk, much to Ruta's dismay.

He took a seat at her long kitchen table which, twice a day—breakfast and supper—was filled with boarders scarfing up her delicious meals.

Ruta, her red, frizzy hair poking out in all directions from under her garish green scarf, poured him coffee, then plunked the pitcher of milk down beside him. "Ye'll have to ruin me coffee yerself." Her Scottish brogue was as strong now as it was the day she arrived many years before.

Ignoring her scorn, Jesse poured milk into his coffee and took a healthy sip without stirring it.

She gazed at him, her mouth forming a moue as she cleared her throat, which meant, Jesse had learned, she was anxious to tell him something. "What is it?"

Ruta sighed, turned away, and fussed with some dishes on the counter. "It's Maybelle."

Jesse straightened. "What about her?"

"Emmeline got word this morning that her sister fell and hurt her knee. She's hoping to go help her with chores until she can manage them herself."

Emmeline and Maybelle were Jesse's aunts who lived in a cabin on the Little Sur River. While Maybelle stayed at the cabin, Emmeline came to help with Jesse's daughter's care.

Gracie Jane was six, his daughter by his ex-wife, an aristocrat who favored her extravagant lifestyle over raising a child who, as a baby, had bad colic. Besides, a one-horse town in California wasn't exactly on his ex-wife's list of places to set up housekeeping. The only good thing that had come out of that union was Gracie Jane. Of course, he might be a bit overprotective when it came to her. Except for her colic, she seemed like a normal, healthy child until she learned to walk, and then she began having pain and swelling in her joints. She spent most days in a wheelchair especially when her pain flared up.

His immediate concern sounded defensive. "Why didn't she come to me?"

"Ye weren't in the office, Jesse."

Damn. He was wrestling an iron skillet from a fuming Margot Pine.

"By the way, she said that awful Lester Johnson shouted obscenities at her from his cell."

"I've told all of you to just ignore him, Ruta. If you don't you just egg him on."

Admittedly, it had been a struggle to keep Gracie Jane with him. She should be in school. He knew that. The local schoolmaster, a dour man with a gray complexion and scraggly hair to his shoulders to match, didn't appear anxious to have another charge in his schoolroom, especially one who couldn't keep up physically with the others. That was fine with Jesse. There had to be another way for his daughter to learn. Neither Emmeline nor Maybelle had a lot of education, but they knew how to read and do their sums, which they had learned early on, just as Jesse had. His ma, Caroline or Sissy, as they all called her, had been a teacher until she got cholera and died when Jesse was eleven. Even when she was ill, she made sure Jesse was learning new things.

He downed his coffee and strode out the kitchen door and into the small apartment Ruta had rented to him. Emmaline was in the 'parlor' as she liked to call it, reading Gracie Jane a story. Gracie Jane, thoroughly enthralled by it, glanced up and caught Jesse's gaze.

"Papa! Auntie Em is reading me a new book, *Little Women*."

Her enthusiasm for everything melted Jesse's heart. His beautiful daughter, with her dark auburn hair and her big brown eyes, reminded him of his own mother. It was always something of a miracle to look at her and, despite her physical limitations, consider her perfect.

His aunt looked up at him. To Gracie Jane, she said, "Honey, try sounding out some words in the story. I need to talk to your pa."

"May I have some tea, Auntie Em? With sugar? It makes me feel all grown up." Happily, Gracie Jane followed her aunt's suggestions, attempting to read the words on her own, her expression riveted to the story.

Emmeline and Jesse went into the small kitchen, and Jesse sat at the table. Em lifted the teakettle off the stove and poured hot water over the tea leaves in the tea pot, then left it to steep before adding the sugar.

"I talked with Ruta," Jesse began. "What happened to Maybelle?"

Emmeline, her dark hair, threaded with gray and drawn back into an immaculate bun, took a cup from the cupboard. "I got a letter early this morning from a runner. Maybelle fell and hurt her knee. She can't walk on it."

If Maybelle was hurt, Emmeline needed to leave immediately. Their new cabin, recently built on old family land, was quite comfortable. Years before, his grandfather had forged a road to the area, although it still wasn't an easy ride. "Go. I'll have Lloyd get the carryall ready. Do you mind if he takes you there?"

"I trust your deputy just fine. I only hope that stubborn sister of mine isn't trying to do too much. It'll only make it worse."

Jesse felt a pinch of guilt at not taking her himself, but Lloyd, although young, was an honorable young man. "Gracie Jane will miss you. We all will."

"Well, maybe later this summer you can bring her out for a while. You know how she loves it there."

What's not to love? A comfortable cabin by a sparkling clean river filled with the most delicious trout a man could ever want. "I might just do that." He didn't voice his concern about Gracie Jane's education. They would get by.

The wood-burning locomotive belched cinders that drummed overhead like hail. Smoke and steam permeated the cars, leaving a thin veneer of grime over everything particularly, Anastasia noticed, her clothing. She thought of closing the window, but the stench of bodies coupled with the smell of whiskey and tobacco made that an unpleasant choice.

Anastasia studied the fleeting landscape from her seat, a hard bench barely wide enough to sit upon and not high enough to rest one's head against. She could have booked a Pullman car, but that would have cost her more, and she had to be careful with her funds.

She'd also heard people talk about their nights in a Pullman.

There was burping and snoring, breaking wind and babies bawling. And, as often as not, someone attempting to crawl into another person's bunk—uninvited. And if you slept in night clothes, changing into them beneath the covers was like trying to undress under a sofa.

She had thought she might draw attention to herself simply because she was alone. Few if any noticed, all being caught up in their own troubles, especially women with children whose husbands had banded together to drink and smoke.

Attempting to close out her abysmal surroundings, she continued to conjure up a plan for her future. She didn't know what questions might come up besides the usual ones, who she was, why she was alone, where she was from. But she had a name ready. Tansy Leigh was born. Leigh was her grandmother's maiden name. No one had spoken of her in years. Tansy was her papa's pet name for her, but since his death, no one had used it. Tansy Leigh's husband died in a farming accident. Thus would begin her web of lies. So far it was easy because she hadn't really spoken with anyone.

She glanced at her hand where the plain, gold ring caught the sunlight. A simple band. A ring her father had worn on his little finger. It fit her middle finger perfectly. Reluctantly she had left a lot of her good jewelry behind. If Oliver were to look inside her Moroccan leather jewel case, he would notice too much missing. That was a bit of a worry anyway because he had bought most of it for her—with her money, of course, although her father had made it impossible for anyone to deplete her trust fund. Something she had learned after her marriage. And something that had put Oliver in a particularly bad mood.

The night of her escape she made sure she had dressed lavishly, wearing some of her finest things, like her gold drop earrings with the diamonds and rubies. She'd left the pearl necklace behind but had worn the bangle bracelet with the rubies and diamonds circling it. Her grandmother's diamond, a three-carat cushion cut extravaganza that Anastasia wore on occasion but felt like a fraud when she did. And her papa's pocket watch. That had been the hardest to leave in Topeka, but she couldn't afford to be sentimental. At the last minute she had shoved the snake-like bangle bracelet into the pocket of her dress. It was nice to get rid of the symbol of her husband, the snake that squeezed the life out of her, like a python in the jungle.

As to the ostentatious ring, Oliver had even commented on it her last evening with him. Frowning, he said, "You never wear that ring. If it were up to me, I'd sell it."

Clarice was touching up her hair, and Anastasia had given him a saccharine smile. "But it isn't up to you, is it?"

His gaze narrowed, and Anastasia was certain that if she hadn't planned her escape for that night, she would have been beaten for such a high-spirited comeback.

Before she had left the house, she gave Clarice a spontaneous hug. She would miss the girl. Anastasia hoped she found a good place to work, for surely Oliver would let her go. She would be the better for it.

A young woman with a wailing infant passed her seat, and Tansy gave her a sympathetic smile. It was not returned. She wondered if women like that ever regretted their choices in life. Maybe they had no choices.

Tansy thought of her mother. She felt dreadful having to put her mother through this—her drowning and her 'death.' Her remorse initially was so strong, she wondered if she could go through with it. And for Sally to think she was gone? That stabbed at her heart daily. Perhaps one day she could rectify things...

Yet here she was, on her way to California. Papa's words still rang true all those years ago.

They had sat together on the porch swing of their lovely estate near Lake Michigan, Papa smoking his pipe. "Nothing like the west coast, Tansy girl."

"Why?" She loved her time alone with him, the smell of his pipe, the gruffness of his voice. His hair, once as dark as her own, was now salted with gray. It distinguished him even further in her opinion.

He chewed on the stem of his meerschaum. "Glorious expanses of fertile land. Wildflowers grow in such abundance they look like carpeting on the hillsides near the ocean."

She tried to imagine it. Carpets of colorful flowers as far as the eye could see. "Is the ocean like Lake Michigan?"

He laughed, his deep infectious laugh, which she loved. And shared. "The Pacific Ocean is considerably bigger than Lake Michigan. The waves crash and roar over the rocks, the spray soars high into the air, reaching for the sky. There's often a rainbow in it. I remember that clearly. Yes," he said wistfully, "California is the prettiest place I've ever been."

He had turned toward her then and added, "They have the biggest and tallest trees in the world right there in California."

Her thoughts returned to the present when the train's whistle screamed. She thought he might approve of what she'd done. He would have listened to her when she complained about Oliver's treatment of her. Papa would have backed Oliver into a corner and threatened him. Oliver might have been a different husband had her papa been alive. But her papa was gone. As always, when she thought of him, there was a raggedy sadness inside her.

"Where did you live when you were there, Papa?"

He had stared out onto the immaculately manicured lawn, his eyes focusing on something far distant. "I was just a lad. Went out with my pal Parnell Cotton." He had looked at her. "You never met Parnell. He was killed in a mining accident, but together we made our fortunes in California, and since he had no kin, everything went to me when he died."

"Was it a town, Papa? Did you live in a town?"

He put his arm behind her, on the back of the swing. "It wasn't a town back then. Just a saloon and a few small businesses. Not much of a town now, either I suspect, but they did go and name it Willow River, because of all the willow trees banked up against the river."

Anastasia had closed her eyes, trying to picture it. Willow

trees were, to her, those beautiful weeping things that made her think of lace. "I wish I could see it one day."

Her papa had patted her on the knee. "Well, I don't much think your mama would appreciate you leaving us and tromping off on your own."

"But you could take me, couldn't you?"

He smiled. She remembered he had looked rather sad. "One day, Tansy girl, you'll learn that a lot of what you do in life isn't exactly what you *want* to do."

Those words had come to pass.

CHAPTER 3

*I*t had been four days. Four days, and no news from the authorities. Anastasia's mother, Grace Jarvis, was pressing for a funeral. Oliver had to admit it; his wife had drowned. The small dingy bringing her out to the yacht had capsized in the waves, and although the young man rowing the little boat had tried to save her, she had gone under and had not come up. There had been an immediate investigation. And of course the grand party that was to have happened on the yacht had to be cancelled. That had upset him because he was to meet with an important contact sometime during the evening. That meeting had yet to be rescheduled.

He still had trouble believing she was gone. The house was empty save for the servants. And quiet. His late wife's booming laugh had always grated on him. Her room had not been touched. Her pearl necklace, one she had decided not to wear, was still in tangles on her dressing table. He lifted it and draped it over the open lid of her jewelry box. Otherwise he didn't touch anything. He didn't dare. Who knew what the authorities would want to look at? And as much as he hoped she was truly gone, he couldn't afford to show it or give the authorities any reason to suspect he'd had anything to do with it.

Grace was beside herself. Sarah and her daughters had arrived the day before. Her presence helped Grace cope. Thank god someone else was around to do it; Grace was a pliable woman, usually bending quickly to his will, but now and then she, too, drove him to want to hit her. Of course he didn't.

What about him? Had he loved his wife? That was almost laughable. But he feigned sorrow whenever asked if he missed her. If she hadn't been an heiress, he wouldn't have given her a second glance. Her position in society was what he valued, for if he would have chosen with his heart instead of his head, he would never have picked her. But he couldn't afford that luxury. She was tall, sometimes graceless, often off in a world of her own and always a bit loud. Not your typical society debutante.

The pen he was holding snapped in two, momentarily startling him just as the swish of Grace's gown announced her presence in the study.

"Well? Have you heard anything?" She appeared dry-eyed. Sarah stood behind her, dabbing at her eyes with a lace handkerchief. She was the beauty of the family. He had often fantasized being with her instead of the cow he had married.

"They have dragged the lake, but the winds were so harsh that night, they fear the…body may have drifted into deeper water."

Grace, a petite woman with fine filaments of silver in her light hair, expelled an impatient sigh and patted the place over her heart. "Thank God the party was cancelled. Even if this tragedy hadn't happened, the weather was unsafe for such a gathering."

"The weather was not the issue. If Anastasia hadn't been late, she would have ridden out with me on the launch instead of climbing into that flimsy dingy. If there's anyone to blame for this, it's Anastasia herself."

Sarah gasped. "Oliver, you don't mean that!"

Oliver composed himself. "No, of course not," he said quickly. "I…I'm just as upset as you are. But if she had just—"

"She didn't," Grace interrupted. "I loved my daughter dearly but sometimes I just didn't understand her. What could possibly have made her late? She's never late. If anything, Anastasia is always early. Unfashionably so. I don't understand it." This time her eyes welled with tears. "I just don't understand it." She crumpled onto the settee and sobbed.

Sarah sat and put a comforting arm around her mother's shoulders, her own tears streaking her cheeks. Oliver couldn't help but notice the curve of her breasts beneath her stylish gown. What a stunning woman she was! He often wondered how the two sisters could be related, then he remembered the old man, Ernest, and realized with a grim smile that Sarah resembled her dainty, pretty mother, and Anastasia was the image of her father.

Grace got control of herself and dabbed at her eyes. "We need to plan the funeral."

"You don't think there's any hope she's alive?" Sarah asked, her voice filled with heartbreaking optimism.

"How could she be?" Her mother all but shouted at her. "What do you think she's doing? Clinging to a life raft? Maybe sitting on some small island in the middle of Lake Michigan, waiting to be rescued? Writing SOS signals in the sand?"

"That would be a long swim," Oliver said under his breath.

"Oh, you know what I mean," Grace snapped.

Sarah rang for tea. Anastasia's maid, Clarice, entered with a tray and tea set. Her eyes were red from crying.

Grace gave her a piercing look. "You didn't notice anything out of the ordinary that night?"

Clarice kept her gaze down. "No, ma'am."

The hard look continued. "What was it that made her late?"

Although Grace had interrogated Clarice earlier, the girl was still upset and shook her head. "Like I said before, I don't know, ma'am. When I left her, she seemed ready to join the others."

Grace motioned the maid to put the tea tray on the table beside her. "Oh, how miserable this is! This is so...so like Anastasia to try my patience."

"Mama, you're not blaming her for her own death, too, are you?" Sarah was aghast.

Grace waved he hands in front of her. "Oh, no. I don't know. But...why did this have to happen? Why?" Her face was marked with despair.

Indeed, thought Oliver. Why had this happened? It was not timely. He wasn't ready.

Leaving the women to make funeral arrangements, Oliver slipped into his Mackintosh, settled his bowler on his head, took his silver handled walking stick, and set out for a walk to the lake.

It was a brisk June day. The breeze off the lake was always cold. His walk took him north along the shore. He stood and studied the spot where the yacht had been moored. He knew that internal waves, or upwellings, often lowered the water temperature near the shore. Had it been so that night? Had the cold taken her quickly?

Until this moment he had not thought of how she might have suffered. But hadn't he heard that drowning was a good way to die, if there was such a thing?

Anger welled up inside him, and he clamped it down. He wasn't ready. Not yet. But he could still take his time. Actually, his life would be more pleasant now that he was playing the grieving widower. As long as he remembered to 'grieve.'

*T*ansy had drifted off to sleep, dreaming she was a little girl and her papa took her hunting astride his horse. The horse had wings. She had asked her papa if the horse could fly, and he had said, "Of course. It's a horse fly."

She was jerked away by the screeching of the breaks. Her neck and back were stiff. If she didn't get up and walk around soon, she'd die of boredom and discomfort. No, she had not expected comfort, but her naiveté had not led her to even consider these appalling conditions. Her traveling suit was covered in soot, as was her hat, she was sure. She was grateful she had packed her cashmere cape in the old travel bag. She, along with everyone else on board, probably looked like they worked at a smithy.

The time it took to reach California seemed like forever, but finally she heard the conductor call out "Willow River," and she became excited. The engine emitted a *shooshing* sound as she made her way to the platform. A noise to her right alerted her to the sound of baggage being tossed none too carefully from the train. She was immediately grateful she had not brought her own expensive leather traveling bag, but her father's which was already beat up and worn. But really, the only reason she didn't take her own was because she didn't want someone to discover it missing. No one missed Papa's old things.

She took in the sight of the town. It was rather quaint. Small buildings, some wood, others possibly adobe, flanked what she presumed to be the main street. Signs hung in front of each shop. The general store, a saloon, the sheriff's office, a small apothecary, and, across the street, a large, white clapboard two and a half story building with a 'room to let' sign.

Although she saw trees in the distance, there were none lining the street. And the street itself was rutted. Dust flew into the air as a lively dog dashed over it. She looked at the sky. How blue it was! Not a cloud to be seen. And the air, although deep into May, was dry. In the breeze there was a hint of some earthy vegetation. How different from the air she'd inhaled the last days on her journey from Chicago! She pulled in a deep breath.

As anxious as she was to see the river, which she had imagined since she was a child, she managed to have her meager possessions held at the station while she looked for a place to stay. The headache she'd acquired during the trip had not abated. Although she'd been sitting for most of the trip, she was anxious to get somewhere, anywhere, other than that horrible train.

Making her way carefully across the rutted road to the rooming house, she held her skirt to keep it from dragging in the dust and then realized that dust on the hem made little difference, since her entire skirt was filthy. She stepped up the wide steps and knocked on the door. A short, round woman with bright frizzy red hair answered. Her cheeks were red and chapped, but her eyes were a startling shade of blue, bright as a robin's egg.

Before Tansy could say a word, the woman grabbed her hands and pulled her inside. Tansy could feel the roughness of her palm against her own. "Ye be needin' a cup of coffee, I'm thinkin'," she announced, closing the door behind her.

Still holding her hand, the woman pulled Tansy along a hallway and into a large, sun-lit kitchen with an enormous table and benches on either side.

"Sit," she ordered. "Ye just got off the train, didn't ye?"

Bemused, Tansy nodded and sat.

"Damn contraption spits so much coal dust I'm surprised we all don't cough up soot."

Tansy glanced at her skirt. "Yes, I'm certainly covered with it."

The woman proceeded to put together a plate of meats and cheeses along with huge chunks of coarse bread. She plunked them down in front of Tansy and followed with a mug of steaming coffee.

She stood back, her fists on her ample hips, and said, "Eat."

Admittedly, Tansy was starving, but she tentatively took a piece of cheese and bit into it. It was smooth and rich and a little tart. It was delicious.

The woman chuckled. "Thought ye wouldn't like it, didn't ye?"

"I…I'm just a little surprised," Tansy answered. "I haven't seen cheese like this before."

"Sheep."

Tansy raised her eyebrows. "Sheep?"

"It's made from sheep's milk," she answered.

Tansy took a chunk of bread, topped it with the meat and a piece of cheese, and took a big bite. Her stomach was singing hallelujah as it accepted the food, and she began to feel better.

The woman sat down across from her, the bright green scarf a bit askew as it attempted to cover her hair. "When ye got off the train ye looked a bit bewildered, but I'm glad ye came directly across the street to me."

"I saw the sign in your window."

Those bright blue eyes lit up. "Ye be lookin' for a place to stay then?"

Tansy took a sip of coffee and coughed as she detected a decidedly strong taste of whiskey. She swallowed anyway, and that, along with the food, helped her feel even better.

"I am, indeed," Tansy answered.

The woman looked puzzled. "Ye be meetin' someone?"

After swallowing another bite of bread, Tansy said, "No. I'm a widow, you see. And I needed a change of scenery. My…my late husband had visited California many years before we were married, and he spoke so highly of it." Tansy gave a little shrug. "I guess I thought it wouldn't hurt to check it out for myself."

"Ye be brave to be travelin' around on your own."

Tansy glanced at the plate in front of her, wondering if she dared finish everything. "I suppose I am. But I've always had a bit of a restless spirit."

Nodding, the woman stuck her hand out. "I'm Ruta Ives, and the room is yours, if ye want it."

Tansy took the roughened hand with the gnarled knuckles in hers. "Tansy," she said. "Tansy Leigh. And yes, I would like the room very much."

Ruta stood. "Follow me. It ain't fancy, but it's clean."

Tansy followed the little, round woman out of the kitchen and up a flight of stairs. At the top she flung a door open and stood aside so Tansy could enter. It wasn't fancy. Tansy didn't think she'd ever seen anything so plain. For a brief moment she thought of the opulence she'd left behind. Had she taken it for granted? Now, looking at the sparsely furnished room that was to be hers, did she miss the grandeur? Would she?

She bit down on her lip as she studied the room. It was clean and brightly lit by the sunshine streaming in through the window. There was a bed with an iron bedstead and a colorful handmade quilt, a small chest with drawers against the far wall on top of which was a plain jug and bowl.

Her glance went to the corner, where a chamber pot stood, discretely hidden by a small wicker divider. She took a deep breath, inhaling sharply. Yes, she would miss her new flush toilet!

As if reading her mind, the landlady said, "There's a necessary out back, but it's not convenient during the night."

A 'necessary', Tansy thought. How rustic. But what had she expected? A simple wooden wardrobe completed the humble decor. A large, round rug lay centered in the middle of the floor. Tansy hadn't seen anything like it before; it appeared to be made of rags. It was...quaint.

All right, this would take some getting used to. Perhaps she hadn't thought this far ahead, but she was here now and would make the best of it. She stopped to assess her feelings. Was she disappointed? No, merely a little surprised, probably at her naiveté.

All of her planning had been for one purpose: to get away

from Oliver. The rest was something she hadn't thought upon. She could stay here or leave. But this was her destination. Her papa's words still lingered in her mind, for it was indeed beautiful here. She would manage day by day and should something else turn up that was more appealing, she would leave.

Realizing the landlady was waiting for her to say something, she turned and gave the woman a friendly smile. "It's lovely, really." When the woman quoted her the weekly price, Tansy hesitated only briefly before agreeing. How long would her money last?

She asked the landlady about retrieving her belongings from the station and was told that it would be taken care of immediately.

When she was alone, she went to the bed and sat on it. The lively quilt was a beautifully hand sewn cluster of odd shapes and sizes of fabric. The colors were extraordinary. Vivid blues, yellows and rosy reds with a forest green border. Certainly she would be cozy under it. She hoped to convince herself that she would not miss her feather down comforters and expensive sheets. And, she thought with a wry twist of her mouth, all of the luxuries she had taken for granted all of her life.

Her belongings arrived, and she put things away, careful of the doll she'd taken with her on a whim.

She picked it up and ran her fingers over the delicate face, and the big blue eyes that opened and shut. She lightly stroked the dark brown hair, which she had kept herself from combing even as a girl. Sally had not been so precise. Her doll's hair was a tangle of knots. Perhaps it had been foolish to pack such an awkward item, but again, she'd had it since she was a girl. A gift from her father. There was so much she had to leave behind; she couldn't leave her doll, but for the life of her, she didn't know why she kept it. It would have been smarter to keep his pocket watch.

When she'd emptied the battered leather travel bag, she stored it in the wardrobe and then went to the window. Her room faced the back of the building. From the second story she could just glimpse the willows that her father had said banked the river. She smiled, recalling how she had envisioned them as weeping, like those in their yard back home. But they were nothing like she'd imagined. Short, rather squat, she guessed they were willows, nevertheless.

Her last swim had been a difficult one despite the fact that she was in good shape. Papa had seen to it that she swam regularly. She had discovered that one of the members of his club had an indoor pool at his residence. She was always welcome to use it, and she had, even after Papa passed. Although she was certain to keep that information from Oliver.

She crossed to the small mirror above the chest and—"Holy Mackerel!" It was an expression her papa had always used when he was surprised. And she was really surprised!

She was soot laden from head to foot! Her face was so dirty that she would probably have frightened young children! She tossed a glance at the dry sink but didn't think there was enough water in the pitcher to begin to clean her up. She wanted to swim. She was grimy and sticky and was sick to death of the clothing she had worn after she'd swum to safety. In very little time at all, she was in her black and white striped knitted wool swimsuit. She picked up her bathing cap but tossed it on the bed. Her hair needed a good washing. She grabbed a bar of soap from the top of the dry sink, threw her cape around her shoulders, and headed out, quietly taking the stairs to the back door.

It was heavenly! The water was cool but not cold and so clear she could see all the stones and bits of growth at the bottom of the river. Minnows wiggled about in the stream, occasionally nibbling at her toes. She quickly immersed herself and washed her hair and face, sinking deep to rinse. After washing every part of her body she could reach, she tossed the soap onto the shore. She took some long strokes that took her downstream, turned a somersault and began swimming against the flow, her arms a little stiff from lack of use. She dove under and pushed herself up from the bottom, springing into the air and then crashing into the river again.

She did it again, and again, and finally she couldn't contain herself. When she sprang into the air, she let out a "whoop!" of pleasure before sinking back under the water.

Suddenly an arm came around her shoulders and pulled her up, out of the water, startling her so that she yelped and tried to pull herself loose. Her attacker held her fast. My god, he was drowning her! She grabbed at the arm, clawing at it, trying to free herself, finally able to get her teeth around his forearm.

Her attacker swore and pushed her under water where she unintentionally swallowed a mouthful.

She lunged upward, breaking the surface, coughing and gasping, trying to rid herself of the water in her lungs.

"Stop struggling!" The male voice was deep and commanding.

She kicked at him, trying to find a place that would cause him to lose his grip on her. She fought and gasped and continued to kick until he gently slapped her face, stunning her so that she stopped.

Enraged, she pummeled him with her fists. By God no man was going to smack her around ever again! "Get away from me, you big ape!"

"I'm trying to save you!"

She pushed against him harder, catching her breath. "I wasn't drowning, you dolt. I was swimming and…and minding my own business!"

They both staggered to the edge of the river, when her 'rescuer' sputtered a line of curses. "Swimming? What sane person goes swimming in this river?"

She hunted for her cape, but it wasn't where she had left it. Hugging herself, she said, "What's wrong with this river?"

He gave her a quick glance and muttered another curse. "This river is a thief. Every year at least one person drowns doing something stupid like you just did. And it's full of snakes."

Despite her condition, she laughed. Snakes. Now, wasn't that just perfect? She'd escaped one snake only to perhaps be bitten by another. She started to shiver but stood her ground.

"You think getting bitten by a snake is somehow funny, ma'am?" He frowned at her, and she couldn't help noticing that his eyes were a deep brown.

"Not under the circumstances," she answered, "I was thinking of another snake." She shivered more. "If the river is dangerous, why isn't there a sign or something?"

"Most of us around here know better than to risk it." He studied her for a moment, and then asked in a perturbed tone, "Who in the hell are you?"

Hoping her teeth wouldn't chatter, she answered, rubbing her arms to warm them, "I really doubt that's any of your business."

"I make it my business." He wiped his forearm. "And you bit me."

She glanced over. His arm was muscular and covered with burnished gold hairs. "I didn't even draw blood." Feeling cold and wet and cranky, she said, "And anyway, you slapped me."

"You were becoming hysterical."

"Yes, because I thought you were drowning me." She gave him a sharp look. "Just who are *you*, might I ask?"

He glanced down at his soggy clothing, and her gaze followed. There, attached to his shirt pocket, was a badge.

"So it's illegal to swim in the river?"

He tossed her a grumpy glance. "There's no law against it."

"Then I will swim here whenever I choose to and risk being bitten," she responded. Her teeth were beginning to clatter against each other.

He threw up his hands. "Don't say you haven't been warned. Go ahead and drown yourself."

She stepped from one foot to the other, attempting to get warm. "I was *not* drowning. I was enjoying a simple swim until you came along. Oh, never mind." How many times did she have to explain herself? She looked around again for her cape. "And I had a wrap with me. It was blue wool. I put it on that big rock, and now it's gone." She looked for the soap. It was nowhere to be seen either. It was probably halfway to the ocean by now, if indeed that's where this river led.

He finally realized she was shivering. He lifted a leather jacket off a tree limb and tossed it at her. "Cover yourself. And I want my jacket back." He turned to go, then spun around again. "And who the hell are you anyway?"

She gratefully slid her arms into the sleeves of the coat. The leathery material smelled of sunshine and something personal she couldn't identify. "If you must know, I'm staying at the rooming house with Mrs. Ives." She truly looked at him for the first time and saw that even wet, his dark hair was shimmering with gold. He was big and tan and had a brawny look about him. And those eyes—a glorious brown. Like the depths of a pot of coffee.

He took her arm, which she shrugged off. He backed away, his palms up in defense. "Don't fret, ma'am, I'm just going to see that you get back to the house safely." He looked her up and down and then added, "We don't get many near naked ladies in these parts. Wouldn't want anything to happen to you."

Trying not to snarl at him, she allowed him to assist her through the willows and the brush for the ground was uneven and rocky. As they approached the back porch of the boarding house, she heard a loud wolf whistle. A few steps to her right stood a young man with a cocky smile. She ignored him.

"On your way, Lester," the sheriff ordered, but not before the young man whistled again and ogled her so blatantly that she blushed. At the steps of the porch, she shrugged off the sheriff's touch, letting his jacket fall to the ground. "I'll be fine. Thank you...I guess, although again, I was not drowning."

The sheriff slapped his hat against his thigh, picked up his jacket, and turned to leave. As she started up the steps, she turned and saw him gawking at her. She hoped he got a good look, because it was the last one he would ever get. She hurried along.

Ruta Ives was waiting for her on the top step. "Good lord, girl, what are ye wearin'?"

"I took a swim." She glanced at the retreating back of the sheriff. "Your law man thought I was drowning and jumped in to rescue me."

Ruta smiled. "Jesse Wolfe. He'd do that, ye know, help a lady in distress. Besides that, he's got a sizeable bag of tricks inside those jeans."

Had she heard the woman right? Certainly not. Tansy was ushered inside where Ruta handed her a bath sheet. "I wasn't in distress. I was just swimming." She was getting tired of explaining herself.

"Well, whatever ye was doin', ye'd best get out of them wet whatever ye call 'ems." She waved a work worn hand toward Tansy's wet, saggy suit.

Tansy thanked her landlady for the towel and made her way up the stairs to her room. She did wonder, however, what had happened to her cape.

Jesse ran a couple of errands and then headed straight back to the boarding house. He found Ruta peeling potatoes for the evening meal. She gave him a sly glance. "Can't figure out why ye're here this time of day, Jesse."

Jesse settled himself at the table. "Who is she?"

"I don't know any more than ye do," Ruta answered.

"You mean you just rented her a room?" He cursed. "She could be running from the law, for god's sake."

Ruta chuckled. "Sure, now, Jesse, yer imagination is running away with ye."

"And she hasn't told you why she's here? Does she know someone in town?" Try as he might, he couldn't get the picture of her backside out of his head as she strolled toward the porch. Hell, the way that suit clung to her, she may as well have been naked. He tamped down that ridiculous ping of need.

Ruta put down her knife and turned to him. "Like I said, I don't know any more than ye do. But," she added, tossing a quick glance toward the stairs, "she had a battered travel bag and very few clothes."

"And?"

Ruta scooted onto the bench across from him. "It's a puzzle,

I'll admit. On the one hand, she seems polished, like a real lady. On the other hand, she ain't got much more with her than a traveling gypsy. She did give me her name...Tansy Leigh."

Jesse smacked the table with his palm. "What kind of woman appears out of nowhere, rents a room, and then takes a swim in that thieving river? Makes absolutely no damned sense to me."

"Why don't ye ask her why she's here?"

"I already did. I asked her after I pulled her out of the river. She wasn't anxious to answer any questions."

"It's likely she'll talk to me, a wee bit, anyway." She glanced at the watch pinned to her blouse. "Time to get Gracie Jane up. She's been restin' for a spell now."

Jesse stood. "Wish I could do it, but I've got to make a call on one of the ranchers on the south end of the river bend." He glanced at Ruta. "You sure this isn't just adding more work to your load?"

Ruta stood as well and returned to the sink. "She's a little darlin'."

Jesse studied her. That wasn't what he'd asked her.

CHAPTER 5

*T*ansy followed the aroma of something so delicious it made her mouth water. She stepped into the kitchen just as Mrs. Ives was taking a batch of cookies out of the oven. They smelled like her favorites that Cook used to make weekly, just for her: Molasses.

"Can I have one now?"

It was a chirpy little voice, that of a child. Tansy glanced around the kitchen and saw a girl sitting at the end of the long table. She was a pretty little thing with dark mahogany curls and big brown eyes. A young boy, perhaps ten or eleven years old, stood by the back door.

"Not until they cool a bit. Ye don't want tae burn yer mouth. And Davey, ye just wait a minute, and I'll have a plate for you to take to your ma and pa."

Tansy cleared her throat.

All three turned and looked at her. The landlady smiled, acknowledging her, the boy hung his head and studied his scuffed shoes, and the little girl stared at her in awe.

"Who are you?" Her voice had a musical lilt to it.

Tansy sat down at the end of the table. "My name is Tansy. What's yours?"

"I'm Gracie Jane Wolfe, and I'm six. My daddy is the sheriff."

Ah, thought Tansy. Her 'rescuer.' "Gracie Jane? Why that's my mama's name. Grace."

"I'm not just Grace. My whole and complete name is Gracie Jane Whitman Rhodes Wolfe."

"That's quite a long name for such a little girl."

"My papa's name is Wolfe. The other two names are from my mama."

Ruta interrupted. "Here you go, Davey, all tucked on the plate with a cloth over them. Tell your ma she can return it whenever she gets a chance."

The boy, whose hair was a handsome shade of rust, thanked the landlady, grabbed the plate, and hurried out the back door.

Ruta explained. "He lives down by the river with his ma and pa." She clucked her tongue. "Don't rightly know how to explain them two," she added.

"The boy's parents?"

The landlady snorted. "Ye'd think they hated each other the way they go at it. But get them separate and they're friendly as anybody. And if Bert was a Scotsman, he'd have to wear a kilt for he's too big fer his britches."

Another odd comment, but Tansy let it pass. She turned her gaze toward the girl. "Does your mama live here too?"

"Oh, no," she said breezily. "My mama lives far away and is very busy and hardly ever visits us."

"I see," Tansy replied, but clearly did not, growing uncomfortable with the direction of the conversation. "So, Gracie Jane, do you go to school?"

Gracie Jane shook her head. "I can't, you see, because I get these pains in my legs, and most times I can't even walk. And here," she added, pulling up the sleeve on her frock, "sometimes I get these sores, and they have to put oatmeal on them so they don't itch too much. I'm not to scratch them, you see."

"Well, that's a lot to think about for such a little girl. You must be very smart."

"Oh, I am. Papa makes sure I learn things. And...and when Aunty Em was here, she started reading *Little Women* to me. But she had to leave and now I don't know what's happening with all those sisters."

A little movement occurred in Tansy's chest, something akin to sadness. "That's one of my favorite books," she answered. She had been reading it to her father the night he died. "And who is Aunty Em?"

Ruta turned from the counter. "Aunty Em is Jesse's aunt, Emmeline Wolfe. She's been helping with Gracie Jane, but her sister had an accident so she had to leave."

"Oh, I hope it isn't serious," Tansy said.

"They're a couple of strong women, although ye wouldn't know it to look at 'em. I guess Maybelle twisted her ankle or knee and can't get all the chores done."

"Do you have a sister?" Gracie Jane asked.

"I do, indeed," Tansy answered.

"I wish I had a sister," Gracie Jane said, a bit forlornly. "What's your sister's name?"

"Sarah. But I always called her Sally." Suddenly realizing she was giving information she should keep to herself, she added, changing the subject, "Maybe I could read *Little Women* to you."

Gracie Jane clapped her hands. "Oh, could you?" She turned to the housekeeper. "Can she, Ruta? Please?"

Ruta frowned, her hands once again on her hips. "Well, I don't s'pose it would do any harm."

"I have the book right here." She dug into a pocket on the side of her chair, and Tansy realized the girl was in a wheelchair. A sharp feeling of pity rose in her chest.

"Well, it's a nice, sunny day, Gracie Jane. Why don't we go out on the back porch and read?"

Gracie Jane's eyes were big. "Outside?" She turned to Ruta. "Can we go outside?"

Ruta appeared uncomfortable. "Well, yer papa don't like you outside too much unless he's with ye."

Tansy thought that was a curious restriction. From her earliest memories, her nannies had wheeled her out into the open air even if there was snow on the ground.

"Well, I s'pose if we put a wrap on ye and cover yer wee legs with a blanket…"

While the housekeeper went to get the wrap, Gracie Jane asked, "Do you have any children?"

"No, I'm afraid not. But I have two nieces who live far away. I don't get to see them often enough."

"What's a niece?"

"Remember my sister, Sally? My nieces are her daughters."

"How old are they?"

Ruta returned with a blanket and a shoulder wrap. "Now, Gracie Jane, don't ask the lady so many questions. And before ye go out, ye need a snack." Ruta Ives put a glass of milk and a plate with two molasses cookies on the table in front of the child.

"But truth to tell," Ruta began, "I've been a might curious about ye meself."

"I imagine you have," Tansy replied. "And I certainly don't want to sound mysterious." She paused and collected her thoughts. "I told you I am widowed."

"Yes, I'm so sorry to hear that," Ruta answered.

"He had been in an accident on our farm, an accident that crippled him and…and eventually took his life."

Ruta pulled a small bowl from under the counter and plopped it on the table. From a tin on the countertop she scooped out a small amount of flour, some water, and something that resembled a yeasting compound. She mixed the ingredients with her hands, forming it into a small ball. "So ye be a farmer's wife, then?"

Well, that was rather a faux pas. What did she know about farming? "Why, yes. But long before we met, he was in California where he'd stopped over for a night in a quaint little town and decided to stay a month, working in the mines. That little town was Willow River."

Ruta covered the bowl with a cloth and set it by the stove. "Well, I've been here more years than I can count. Mebbe I knew him."

Tansy felt herself blush. "Oh, like I said he wasn't here long, and he spent most of his time in the mines."

"What was his name?"

Yes, Tansy, what was his name? "Leigh. John Leigh. Actually, it was Johan, but since coming to America, he insisted on being called John." *Don't get too creative.*

"Don't ring a bell. So he come over from Germany, did he?"

"Yes, yes, Germany," Tansy said, thinking quickly.

"Well, I'm sorry for your loss. Now, can I bring ye something else to eat? Imagine that swim took some wind out of yer sails."

Tansy pressed her hand to her stomach. "I'll admit that. Can you hear my stomach growl from where you are?"

Gracie Jane, who had devoured both of her cookies, giggled.

"Nope, but I'm thinkin' coffee isn't what you need. You need a big glass of cold buttermilk."

Tansy stopped herself from making a face. Buttermilk? Only poor farmers and their hired hands drank buttermilk. At least that's what she heard! She swallowed. "Coffee will be fine, thank you. Don't bother yourself."

"Tisn't no bother. It's fresh and sweet and with a couple of molasses cookies, you'll feel satisfied." She took a pitcher from a large cooler and poured a big glass full. She put it on the table in front of Tansy.

Tentatively, Tansy lifted it to her lips and inhaled. Expecting to smell the sharp, acidic smell of the buttermilk she was familiar with, it was indeed sweet. She took a sip. It was very refreshing. "I thought it was made with sour milk."

"Oh, some is. I use fresh milk to make butter and skim off what ye be drinking."

Tansy all but guzzled it down.

The late afternoon air was fresh and clean, smelling of honeysuckle and wild grapes. Bees hummed in and amongst the flowers, and a tiny hummingbird searched for nectar. In the distance she could see the outline of the mountains, tall, granite, and majestic, against the skyline. The town wasn't at sea level. She wondered what the elevation was.

While she got both of them situated, she said, "Miss Alcott was quite an incredible woman. I'll bet you didn't know she was a nurse in the war."

"I thought she wrote books."

"Of course she did." That was really all the information a six-year-old wanted to know so she sat on a chair beside Gracie Jane, opened the book and said, "Shall we start at the beginning?" She glanced down at the cover. *Little Women or Meg, Jo, Beth and Amy. By Louisa May Alcott.* Yet another blast of memories washed over her.

"'Christmas won't be Christmas without any presents,' grumbled Jo, lying on the rug.'"

She had barely gotten into the first chapter when she heard a shout.

"Hey! What are you doing?"

She glanced up to find the sheriff looming over them. His meaty fists were on his hips which pulled his shirt tight across his chest. At his throat she saw a tuft of dark hair.

She calmed herself. "What does it look like I'm doing?"

He took the handles of the wheelchair and spun Gracie Jane around, heading for the door.

"But, Papa," she pleaded, "she was reading to me."

He shouted for Ruta, who came and rolled Gracie Jane inside, and then he rounded on Tansy.

"She is not to go outside without my permission," he growled.

Standing to face him, Tansy asked, "And why is that? It's a beautiful day. Every person alive needs fresh air and sunshine."

His jaw clenched. "In case you hadn't noticed, she isn't well."

Tansy raised her eyebrows. "Because she has pains in her joints?"

"Yes," he snapped. "And…and bad patches on her skin that are irritated by the sun."

Tansy threw up her hands in defeat. "I apologize. But I don't understand what harm fresh air and sunshine could have on her as long as she's covered up."

He paced the porch. "She could catch something out here."

"Like what, a whiff of lilacs? The scent of ruby ripe grapes?"

He frowned at her. "Who are you, again, and why in the hell are you here, meddling in my business?"

Refusing to repeat her story, she answered, "If you want to know about me, ask Mrs. Ives. I have told her why I'm here." With that, she swished past him, opened the door, and made sure to slam it hard behind her.

Jesse waited a few moments before going inside. Hopefully she was gone. He really didn't want to face her again. He'd rarely heard such sarcasm from a woman. It wasn't feminine. Even his ex-wife with all of her failings, had not been sarcastic, at least not in the beginning.

Ruta and Gracie Jane were in the kitchen, waiting for him. Ruta apologized for her role in the misadventure.

He raked his fingers through his hair. "Maybe I over reacted, but you know how I feel about her being out without me."

Ruta put a fresh glass of buttermilk in front of him. "I know, but it seemed so right. Gracie Jane was bored. Miss Tansy was eager to entertain her. I didn't think it would do any harm."

"Miss Tansy"?

"That be her name. The widow Leigh, if you must know." She went on to explain to him what Tansy had told her.

He shook his head. "I still think it's odd for a woman to travel alone, widowed or not."

"Well, she ain't no delicate flower, if ye ask me," Ruta said under her breath.

Jesse agreed. No normal woman puts on flimsy bathing attire and swims in a strange river. And he didn't think he was all that sheltered, but he had never, ever seen a woman outside, in the daylight, who was practically naked. That picture would never leave his mind no matter how hard he tried. And for god sake, there could have been snakes in there. "I still wonder why she came here."

"I told you why," Ruta answered.

"To end up here? Where she doesn't know anyone?"

"Because her mister had said it was beautiful. Ye are just too suspicious, Jesse."

He drained the buttermilk and slammed the glass on the table. "That's why I'm the sheriff."

Ruta cleared her throat.

"Now what?" Jesse asked.

"Well, she don't seem to have much. Mebbe she needs something to do to keep herself busy. She did pay for the room, but I noticed how carefully she counted out the coins."

"You want me to have her clean out the cells down at the jail?"

"Don't be cheeky. Mebbe she could..." Her gaze went to Gracie Jane, who was totally immersed in their conversation.

"What?" Jesse stood so fast the bench toppled over behind him.

"Papa! Don't yell!" Gracie Jane put her hands over her ears and closed her eyes.

"Sorry, honey." Jesse righted the bench and started pacing.

"The woman's smart. Even ye can see that. And she was good with the girl, Jesse. What's the harm in askin'?"

To have that woman under foot day after day? If anything, it would harm his mental state. She purely annoyed the hell out of him. He wasn't sure why. But Gracie Jane did need a tutor.

He stopped in front of the window and stared out over the back lawn, down to the river where the willows wafted in the wind. "I suppose you could ask her."

"Me?" Ruta snorted. "It's up to ye, Jesse. Swallow yer pride, or whatever it is that's eatin' at ye, and ask her yerself."

He went to the door. "I need to get back to the jail. If it's no trouble," he added, a bit cynically, "ask her to meet me there in the morning."

———

The following morning, Tansy opened her eyes. *Where...?* She rubbed her eyes and studied the ceiling, initially confused at her surroundings. Then she remembered, relaxed, snuggling deeper under the quilt. No Oliver to contend with. No beating because she didn't behave as he expected. The person she was inside was not someone's punching bag. Why had she allowed it to go on so long? Probably because of her mother. "Never, ever air your dirty laundry." Her mother's voice, scolding her when, as a girl, she'd accidently repeated something she'd heard in the kitchen, where she shouldn't have been in the first place.

But she had loved the big, warm kitchen with all of the delicious smells. And Cook always did something special for her, telling her it was their secret. No one else needed to know. And yes, she often heard things her youthful ears shouldn't have, but it was almost like she was invisible, for the help simply gossiped around her. Oddly, one of the things she would miss the most was the visits to the kitchen.

She had few friends her age. Most of them were like Sarah, eager to do what was expected of them, tiny, feminine, bursting with the joy of becoming like their mothers. Tansy had long since realized she preferred her father's company over anyone else's, so when he died, she felt very lonely indeed.

She slid from the bed and braved the chamber pot, then dug into her bag for a fresh bar of soap and washed herself in the basin. She put on a fresh, although wrinkled dress but couldn't do much with her hair. She attempted to pull it back and away from her face. The night before, when the landlady had told her about the sheriff's request, she thought of nothing else until she fell asleep. What could he possibly want from her? Did he want her to leave so he wouldn't have to drag her drowning body from the river?

But dinner was interesting, and she met the other boarders, all men, who were, she could tell, on their best behavior. The most interesting tenant, Zeb Parker, was a lawyer, once very acclaimed, she'd been told by Ruta, but now played poker and drank away his days. Even so, he was very interesting and knowledgeable and probably had been a fine solicitor.

And then of course, there were the brothers, Will and Walt Pederson, neither of whom had ever married, and both bragged they'd dodged a bullet by being single. They weren't twins, but it was hard to tell them apart. Both tall, gangly, bald with enormous gray beards and so bow-legged one would have thought they were raised on horseback. Their faces were lined; their skin looked like the skin of a turtle.

Before checking herself in the tiny mirror over the wash basin, she retrieved the travel bag and checked the secret pocket. Her money was still there. The train had made a long stop in Topeka, and she'd been able to sell most of her jewelry. She knew she wouldn't get what it was worth, but what she did get would last her quite some time. She left her room and made her way downstairs. It was early enough that she found herself alone in the kitchen with the landlady.

"Good mornin'. How'd ye sleep?" Ruta poured Tansy a mug of coffee and set it in front of her.

The aroma was lovely, and when Ruta placed a plate of fresh, hot biscuits in front of her, she was ready to eat. "The bed is quite comfortable. I slept well."

"Got some milk gravy to go with them biscuits, but I—"

"Oh, that sounds glorious," Tansy interrupted.

With a big smile, Ruta set a bowl of gravy in front of Tansy. "Glad ye got a good appetite."

Tansy poured gravy over her biscuits, cut into one and took a bite. "Um. These are heavenly. And I've always had a good appetite, just ask..." She glanced up at Ruta. "Just ask anyone," she finished lamely.

She left the boarding house with a light shawl over her shoulders and walked to the jail. When she stepped inside, the sheriff was going over some papers. He barely glanced up at her.

"Have a seat," he offered, tossing his arm toward a chair.

"Am I under arrest?"

He glared at her, ignoring her question, and said, "You're an educated woman?"

"Oh, God," she murmured. "Is that illegal here too?"

"What?"

"Well, it seems to be illegal to swim in your river, so I assume

47

it's also illegal for women to have an education in your quaint little town."

He leaned forward, put his elbows on the desk. "I never said it was illegal to swim in the river, I simply said it wasn't safe." He paused and studied her. "So, what's eating you, anyway?"

She bristled. "Me? What's eating me? I think you should ask yourself the same question."

He threw up his hands in surrender. "All right, let's just say that for some reason, we might have gotten off on the wrong foot."

"Like you trying to rescue me from drowning even though I've been swimming quite capably since I was four?"

His response was a low growl, deep in his throat.

She waited.

"My daughter needs tutoring."

Surprised, she sat up and gave him a serious look. "A teacher?"

"I do believe that's the same thing, isn't it?"

Tansy bit the inside of her cheek. Such a cynical man! "You're offering me a position as Gracie Jane's teacher?"

"That about sums it up, if you're qualified."

Was she qualified? She'd had the best education a young woman could have. Private schools. Private tutors. Surely she'd learned something! "I believe I'm as qualified as anyone you could find, sir."

"Good. Start today. We can discuss your pay later, if that's all right with you." With that he stood, deftly avoiding a lantern that hung over the desk, indicating their little meeting was over.

CHAPTER 6

*G*race and Oliver had Tansy's jewelry box between them at the table.

"I can't find the ring. It was my mother's," Grace explained.

"Oh, that. She was wearing it the night she…" Oliver glanced away to avoid Grace's eyes.

"You mean it's at the bottom of Lake Michigan?" Grace sniffled. "I thought perhaps one of the servants had taken it."

"There are a few other pieces missing. Maybe you can blame the servants for their disappearance."

Grace rifled through the drawer. "And the pearls? Where are the pearls?"

Oliver thought a moment. "They're draped over the back of the case." He pulled them down and handed them to her. "At least she wasn't wearing these. As it is, a good share of the expensive things is gone."

Grace harrumphed. "She rarely wore jewelry at all. Why is it that one particular night she chose to wear the most expensive pieces we owned?" Grace worked her fingers over the pearls, as if they were worry beads or a rosary, and glanced at the dressing table. "Where's her silver handled brush?"

"Maybe her maid took it." He had let Clarice go shortly after the accident. God knew how much she'd pilfered before she left.

And he didn't like loose ends. He hadn't grilled her sufficiently. Did his wife confide in her? Was she aware of how his wife got her bruises?

He stood and went to the bedroom window. The lawn stretched out far to the back, near the woods. The trees were going to be changing soon. And he wanted to get on with his life. Tie up all loose ends. Find another...victim. "You knew your daughter better than I did."

"Oh, Oliver, I didn't know her at all! She was her father's daughter in every way." Grace dabbed at her eyes. "I told her more than once she should have been a boy." Tears welled up. "Oh, why couldn't she have been more like Sarah? I understand Sarah. I never understood Anastasia, and I imagine it displeased her. I...I wasn't the right mother for her, you know."

That much was true. Although Anastasia had never reacted to her mother's lack of interest in her as she was, Oliver had occasionally seen sadness in her eyes. Only once he remembered her saying anything, and then it was simply, "Why can't she accept me the way I am?"

But it had nothing to do with him. His wife's happiness was not his concern. And he doubted his wife was displeased when compared to her father. She seemed to revel in any reference that compared her to the pompous, overbearing man.

"On the contrary," he began, "she was happy with the comparisons." How else could he respond? She was neither dainty nor subdued, like her sister. She was, in Oliver's mind, a man in a woman's body. The penchant for hunting, fishing, riding and swimming. The loud, booming laugh. The tall, full, hardly girlish, figure. There were men who appreciated a Rubenesque woman. He was not one of them.

He turned to find Grace studying the bookcase.

"I suppose something should be done about all of her books," she mused. "When Sarah was here, she took some of Anastasia's favorites, but..."

"They're not in anyone's way," Oliver answered. But truthfully, he didn't give a damn if they were thrown into a pile and burned.

It had been a week since she'd begun tutoring Gracie Jane, and Tansy learned that her student was a very quick study. She knew her basic sums and was learning to read. They spent a part of each day reading Little Women. It brought Tansy great bouts of nostalgia.

"Jo is my favorite sister, Miss Tansy. Who is yours?"

Tansy thought a moment. "Jo is practically everyone's favorite sister. Mine, too." She did identify with Jo. They were both tomboys and loved to do anything that was out of the realm of 'normal.'

"And Marmee…" Gracie Jane looked wistful. "She's such a nice mama."

Tansy thought of her own mother, who was mourning her "death," and she felt the sting of tears. It was one thing to fool Oliver, quite another to do this to her mother even though they were at odds most of her life. A line from *Little Women*, some of which she knew line for line, went: "I wish I had no heart. It aches so." She doubted her mother felt that way, but she knew, with a twist of agony in her stomach, that Sally would definitely feel that way.

"Do you have a mama?"

Gracie Jane's question brought Tansy out of her gloomy musings. "Yes, I do."

She felt Gracie Jane's gaze on her face. "Do you miss her?"

All Tansy could do was nod her head. There was a knot in her throat.

"I don't see my mama very much. She's very busy."

Curious, Tansy asked, "Do you miss not seeing her?"

Gracie Jane cocked her head. "I don't know her very well, but I do miss having a mama. Ruta loves me, and I love her, but… she's not my mama. And Aunty Em loves me and so does Aunty May."

"Aunty May?"

"She's Aunty Em's sister. They live in a cabin by a river. It's so peaceful there."

"Do you get to go there often?"

Gracie Jane smoothed the blanket over her knees. "Not as often as I want to. I have to wait until Lloyd can run the town."

"Lloyd?"

"He's Papa's deputy, and he's a nice man." She made a face. "He has a brother, Lester, who is not nice at all."

Tansy raised her eyebrows, remembering the wolf whistle. "Yes, I believe I've met Lester."

Gracie Jane took a deep breath and brushed a curl from her eyes. "Did Sally have a favorite sister?"

Startled, Tansy asked, "Sally?"

"Your sister, Sally. Did she have a favorite sister in the book?"

Tansy wilted a little, realizing again that of all the people she had left behind, her sister was the one she missed most even though they seldom saw one another. They were both avid letter writers, but now…

"Oh, yes. Sally loved Beth." They hadn't come to the part in the book for the girl to raise a question about death.

After their little session, Tansy took Gracie Jane out onto the front porch so they could watch the people go by.

"There's Mrs. Pine," Gracie Jane announced. "Hello, Mrs. Pine!"

Tansy glanced toward the road where a rather pretty woman with reddish hair waved and hurried over.

"Why, if it isn't sweet little Gracie Jane Wolfe. And how are you today, Lady Jane?"

Gracie Jane expelled an impatient huff. "I am not Lady Jane. I am Lady Gracie Jane, Mrs. Pine."

The woman winked and glanced at Tansy. "You must be the new teacher the sheriff hired." She stuck out her hand, and Tansy took it. It was rough and calloused, and she had a firm grip. "I'm Margot Pine. Me and my mister got a cabin down by the river."

Tansy introduced herself as well. "I've seen a young boy around who looks very much like you. Do you have a son?"

She beamed. "I do indeed. His name is Davey. He's a good boy. Will be twelve next month."

They chatted about little things, and soon Margot Pine hurried off, waving and smiling as she left.

"She's a nice lady," Tansy said, watching the woman hustle down the road.

Gracie Jane gave her a sly glance.

"What's that look for?"

Gracie Jane leaned over and said in a voice low and gruff, "Pa says, 'the Pines are going to kill one another one of these days.'"

They sat quietly for a moment, and then, once again, Tansy heard a wolf whistle. She shaded her eyes and saw a young man sauntering their way. Gracie Jane took Tansy's hand and squeezed it, as if in fear.

Lester gave them a cocky look from the grass. "Too bad you ain't wearing that whatchamacallit today, ma'am. It was mighty appealing."

To Tansy's dismay, she started to blush. She had a retort on the tip of her tongue when Ruta came rushing out, slamming the door behind her. "You git, Lester Johnson, or I'll take a broom to yer backside, and I don't mean maybe."

He merely laughed and went on his way, whistling a nonsensical tune.

Later that afternoon, while Gracie Jane was resting in her room, Tansy went to the kitchen for a cup of Ruta's nerve jangling coffee. She raised the question of Gracie Jane's mother.

Ruta was preparing apples for a pie. "Oh, her." Her voice had a decidedly distasteful ring to it. "I don't suppose it matters if you know the truth." She left the pie making a moment and fetched a plate of cookies and put them on the table in front of Tansy.

She took one and without thinking, dunked it into her coffee, just as her Papa had always done. "The truth?"

Ruta rolled out a crust and placed it in a pie tin. "She couldn't be bothered with a child who wasn't perfect. Ya see, even though Gracie Jane didn't start complaining about her knees and ankles 'til she got older, she was a colicky baby. Cried all day and all night. Why, I even had to give her a sugar teat from time to time to calm her down."

"Sugar teat?"

Ruta glared at her. "Ye don't know what a sugar teat is?"

At Tansy's negative response, Ruta said, "a rag soaked in whiskey and sugar."

Tansy dunked her cookie again and took another bite. "Really? You gave a baby whiskey?"

Ruta snorted and planted her fist on her ample hip. "Well, it wasn't as if I poured a glass of it down her throat. Just a little with some sugar to calm her fussy stomach. Once she spewed so hard, the milk came out like a geyser and hit the ceiling."

Tansy finished her cookie, unable to visualize such an event. "I've never heard of such a thing. So, because the baby was fussy, her mother just...up and left her?" This startled Tansy. Even her own mother, with whom she was always at odds, had neither left her nor sent her away! "She...she must have had a reason." Tansy was being generous. There could not be a reason to do such a thing.

"Oh, yes," Ruta answered, sprinkling the apples with sugar and cinnamon, "she was a high-born socialite who couldn't be bothered."

A high-born socialite. Although Tansy seldom thought of herself in those terms, she certainly knew a number of young women who played their roles in society with eagerness and aplomb.

She was invading the sheriff's life, but she had to ask. "What on earth brought the two of them together in the first place?" She didn't know the sheriff very well, but he didn't appear to be the type to tolerate a socialite. He certainly didn't tolerate her, and she suspected he would reject her helping Gracie Jane outright if he knew.

Ruta snorted. "Oh, she come out here playin' like she loved the place, set her cap for Jesse, and he, bein' a young bull, fell hard." Ruta crimped the edges of the crust and sprinkled the top with sugar. "She gushed about everything, but never promised to live here."

"So the sheriff thought she would stay?" Tansy took a sip of the toxic coffee.

"Obviously, or he would never have wed her." Ruta slid the pie into the big, iron oven. "She stayed until Gracie Jane was born, then, when she realized the child was crampy and fussy, she flew the coop.

"Jesse let her get a divorce on abandonment, even though she was the one who did the abandoning."

"Poor Gracie Jane," Tansy said softly.

"Don't pity the child. Jesse loves her enough for two people, and his aunts dote on her when they can. And I don't think Judith has been here more than a half dozen times in Gracie Jane's young life."

Judith. Her mother's sister's name. Everywhere she went her past followed her. "But how does she explain her absences?"

"Oh, Jesse takes care of it. He don't want to make Gracie Jane hate her ma, but he makes it plain that even though the woman is her ma, she simply don't want to live here."

"Does Gracie Jane ever want to go with her when she leaves?"

"I don't know, but I hope it never comes to that."

Just then Jesse walked into the room. "Where's Gracie Jane?" Although he spoke to Ruta, his eyes were on Tansy; his gaze made her uncomfortable.

"She's in her room, lying down," Tansy answered.

"What? You didn't make her rest outside on the porch where she could get attacked by a swarm of wasps?"

Startled, Tansy asked, "Are there wasp nests around the porch?" God, but he angered her. He was the most cantankerous man she'd ever met.

He had the decency to look away, but he didn't respond. When he turned back, his gaze roamed over her briefly. "Will and Walt told me you wanted to know of a good fishing spot."

Ruta snickered. "Them two ain't got a full set of balls between them."

"Now, Ruta," Jesse warned, giving her a harsh glance.

Once again, Tansy was taken aback. Was Ruta really talking about their...private parts?

Will and Walt had emerged from their rooms with poles and fishing paraphernalia earlier that morning.

"Yes," she answered. "I love to fish. It's very pleasant to be out somewhere and not have the nattering of another human being around. It's rather like swimming. Something I like to do alone," she finished with emphasis, her glare fixed on the sheriff.

He rolled his eyes and threw up his hands. "Well, then, have at it."

After he'd gone, she turned to Ruta and said, "He didn't tell me not to take Gracie Jane with me."

Ruta shook her head. "Oh, lord, if the two of ye had horns, ye'd be locked together for eternity, ye both be stubborn as mules." She checked on the pie. "Do ye really enjoy riling him?"

Tansy straightened. "Of course not, but he seems to enjoy sticking needles under my skin."

Ruta smiled and sighed. "Well, I will say things have gotten more interestin' around here since you came."

Tansy guessed that might be a compliment. "I noticed a piano in the parlor. Do you mind if I play?"

"Help yerself, dear. It's probably out of tune. No one has played it since Judith."

"She was accomplished?"

"Pardon my language, but hell yes. Them socialite types can do just about anything that is useless as tits on a bull. Lord knows they ain't trained to do anything useful, in the kitchen or anywhere else. Prob'ly not even the bedroom," she said with a quiet snicker.

Tansy bit the inside of her cheek. "You're judging all socialites by Judith's standards?"

Ruta sputtered through her lips. "Ye seen one, ye seen 'em all."

"I think I'll go try the piano," Tansy answered without further comment.

She sat on the stool and opened the lid. It was a nice piano, not extremely expensive but well finished. She wondered how it ever got here. The keys were finely made and showed little wear.

She played one of her favorite Bach inventions, not surprised to find her mood lifting and her shoulders relaxing.

Someone stepped behind her. She turned and found the lawyer, Zeb Parker, watching her, his pipe between his teeth and his gray, curly hair rumpled. His eyes were bloodshot, and Tansy could smell whiskey.

"You play very well," he said. "Lessons, I presume?"

"Ah, yes. My…father saw to it that I learned to play at a very young age, and it was probably the only thing I enjoyed doing indoors." Her fingers raced over the keys.

He rummaged around on top of the piano and brought out some music. "I guess the only thing any of us miss about Gracie Jane's mama was her playing." He handed Tansy a sheet of music. "She played this for us a lot, and we'd all stand around and sing."

Tansy glanced at the work. Stephen Foster titles. "These are good singing tunes," she agreed.

"Maybe we could have a sing along one night," he suggested, his voice hopeful.

Relieved to do something she actually did well, she agreed.

That evening, after dinner, Tansy sat at the piano and played every Stephen Foster tune, and Zeb, with a rich baritone, sang beautifully. Will and Walt sang their hearts out, but were a tad out of tune, and even Oscar, the recluse who lived on the third floor, came down and sat on the bottom step and slapped his palm on his knee in time to the music.

She was happier than she'd been in a very long time. The only thing that did rile was that she noticed the sheriff lounging against the door frame, watching her the entire time. She'd never met a man like him. And truth to tell, with that thatch of wavy sun-bleached coffee colored hair and those big brown eyes, he was easy to look at. Besides, she thought, hiding a grin, Ruta claimed he had a sizeable bag of tricks. Although Tansy wasn't very experienced along those lines, she had a feeling she knew what it meant.

CHAPTER 7

Journal Entry:
   While the crow has a vocal sound, a nasal caw-caw high pitched sound, the raven's is low and hoarse.
   I have noted that the crow can live up to eight years but the raven can live as long as thirty.

The next morning, on his rounds, Jesse met Margot Pine coming out of the general store. He greeted her, tipped his hat, and was about to walk on when she touched his sleeve.

"Sheriff," she began, "thanks for always coming by and keeping me from clobbering that man of mine."

He was out there generally about once a week. "Things going more smoothly this week?"

She chuckled. "Bert's been under the weather with a terrible cough and a fever. Doc says he has to stay put or else."

Jesse watched as she adjusted the shoulder of her cape. It was a wrap of very fine blue wool. He didn't remember ever having seen it before. "Nice cape, Margot."

She preened. "Davey brought it home one day. Says he found it by the river. No one was around, so he took it and brought it home to me." She glanced at him from beneath her lashes. "Truth to tell, I've never had anything so fine in all my life."

Jesse recalled his first meeting with Gracie Jane's teacher. Hadn't she mentioned that her wrap was missing after they both stumbled out of the river?

Jesse rubbed his neck. "Seems odd that someone would leave such a fine piece of clothing just lying around, don't you think?"

She answered, her expression serious, "Why, yes I did. But Davey promised there wasn't a soul around. He just didn't have the heart to leave it there, I guess."

Jesse nodded, and went on his way. How to handle this? Davey was always picking up other people's things. Jesse didn't know why. He seemed like a perfectly normal boy in other respects. Maybe he should just let it be. And it wasn't up to him to judge another family's child. But yet, it was a form of theft whether Davey looked on it that way or not.

And Davey knew it was wrong. A few weeks ago, when Jesse had spotted the horse blanket, Davey had immediately blushed and hung his head. Now, the cape. When the weather cooled, and it would, the widow Leigh would need her wrap. A couple of months ago it was Ruta's pie, cooling on the porch. It had been a problem for some time. He just wasn't sure how to handle it. And then, slowly, an idea wormed its way into his head.

Tansy flung open the window in her room and drew in deep breaths of fresh, crisp air. The sky, blue as the inside of one her china cups, was cloudless again. Back home, a day could begin blue and cloudless, but by mid-morning clouds crept into the sky, and before a person knew it, they were skimming swiftly over the sun, blocking it out, or just hovering there, making everything grey, including her mood.

This day was too fine to sit indoors and go over boring sums. The sheriff had conceded that taking Gracie Jane out onto the porch was fine on occasion. "Just don't make a habit of it," he said with a dark scowl.

To Tansy, it seemed that after each hour in the outdoors, Gracie Jane perked up. Her cheeks were pink, her beautiful brown eyes sparkled, and she seemed stronger. And when no one was watching, she put the girl's limbs through a range of motion exercise. Even Tansy knew that lack of exercise was dangerous.

She recalled a young boy at home who had leg weakness, and every day a nurse would come by and take him through a routine of exercises. He seemed to improve. Tansy had watched the nurse work one day when she was at the boy's home, speaking with his mother about one of her favorite charities.

Of course, there was no way to know if the two children had similar problems. It would be best just to let things be. But what if exercise could help Gracie Jane? Wouldn't she feel remiss if she did nothing when something could be done? Then again, was it any of her business?

She left her room, and as she took the stairs to the kitchen, she wondered why that sweet little girl had to have such a stubborn father.

On the landing, she met Will and Walt. "Going fishing again, boys?"

"Yep," Walt answered, his lips working over his toothless gums. "Got an extra pole here too, if ya like."

"Oh, my," she began. "It would be lovely…let me give it some thought, all right?"

Walt nodded. "I'll leave it by the door fer ya."

The kitchen was warm and sunny, and Ruta was whipping up something. She turned to Tansy and said, "Apple brown betty." Tansy wasn't sure what that was, but she imagined it was delicious. Last night they'd had a dessert called Indian pudding made from corn meal, sugar, molasses, and spices. Tansy had never had anything like it in her life. "Your work is never done, is it?"

Ruta looked down at the bowl. "Oh, this? This ain't work. This is pure pleasure. But I am falling behind on the laundry. One of the local lassies usually helps, but she's off with her fella today." She glanced at Tansy. "It ain't hard work. Mebbe you could help?"

Tansy raised her eyebrows. *Laundry?* Of course she'd seen it done. She'd even done a bit of folding and sorting before Oliver put a stop to it. Putting on a brave front, she said, "Point the way, and I'll do my best." There was no way to get out of it save to admit who she really was.

"Zeb got the wash tub ready. There's hot water in it. The scrubbing board is there by the back door." She reached under the counter and pulled out a bowl. "Here's the soap. This week it's mostly sheets." She went to the window and pulled aside the curtain. "There's a hollowed out log you can use for rinsing. I use it as a sink. Got water in there already, too."

She reached under the counter again. "And here's some clothes pegs."

Wash tub? Scrubbing board? A log sink? Clothes pegs? She stopped a horse snort of laughter. Goodness, just how hard could it be for a socialite who was 'worthless as tits on a bull'? The first thing she saw when she stepped out onto the porch was the pile of sheets and bedding on the grass. Before she gave it too much thought, she forged ahead, rolled up her sleeves, and pretended she knew what she was doing.

Jesse stepped to the window, next to Ruta. For a moment, they both just stood there and watched. The widow Leigh was fighting with a sheet, pulling it along the grass, trying to pin it to the line. The wind kept whipping it away, and the widow kept struggling with it. Finally, Jesse spoke.

"I'm thinking she hasn't done laundry like this before."

Ruta shook her head. "She was a farmer's wife. How else do they do laundry? Ain't no fancy machines available for most of us."

Jesse scratched his chin and then ran his hand over his stubble. "Does she seem like a farmer's wife to you?"

Ruta shrugged. "There's all kinds, I suspect."

"Have you ever looked at her hands?"

"Why in God's name would I look at her hands?" Ruta asked.

"They're pretty soft for a working woman, especially one who works on a farm."

Ruta gave him a sidelong glance. "Since when do you look at a woman's hands?"

Jesse waved off the question and continued to observe the spectacle out on the lawn. She had finally gotten the sheet pinned to the line, where it flapped in the breeze along with several others. He watched as she wiped her forehead with her sleeve and blew her riotous curls away from her face. She was a decent looking woman. Hell, actually she was quite pretty. If she didn't have such a cantankerous disposition, he might find her attractive.

All the laundry was on the line, and Jesse saw that she was studying the wash tub, probably wondering how to empty it. It was damn heavy. He knew that. He pushed himself away from the window, went to the door, and stepped out onto the porch.

"Need some help?"

She squinted up at him, her face flushed, and her gown wet all the way down the front. "I saw you at the window. Did you enjoy the show?"

He felt a bite of awkwardness. "Laundry isn't my specialty." By the looks of her, he was pretty certain it wasn't hers.

She studied the tub again, and he left the porch and went to her side. "I'll empty this. I imagine you should be with Gracie Jane."

Relieved, Tansy hurried to her room, changed into a dry gown and went to Gracie Jane.

She stepped into the room, and Gracie Jane's first response was, "Your hair is all curly."

"I was doing the laundry," Tansy answered.

"I know. I walked to the window and watched you. Nothing hurts me too much today."

Tansy took the girls hands in hers. "Take some steps for me."

Gracie Jane took a tentative step or two, and then walked to the door and back again. "See?"

"Do you walk for your papa?"

The girl screwed up her face. "Not too much. He worries I'll hurt myself."

It was clear to Tansy that the sheriff was an overprotective father, but then, could she blame him? He was undoubtedly doing what he thought was best for her, even if Tansy didn't agree with him.

Gracie Jane tilted her head to one side. "Your hair looks pretty that way."

Tansy put her hand to her head. Her mother never thought her hair was anything but an uncontrollable mop when it was like this. "I should go and fix it."

"No," Gracie Jane pleaded. "I wish you'd wear it that way all the time."

It would be easier, wouldn't it? Not having to constantly tame it into a presentable chignon. "Well, the morning is nearly gone. What shall we do until lunch?"

Gracie Jane gave her a sly look and pulled a book from the side of her chair.

Tansy grinned. "*Little Women* it is." She discovered that reading it brought her calming memories from home despite the constant twinge of sadness.

"And, Miss Tansy? I heard you playing the piano. Could you teach me?"

"What a wonderful idea! Yes, indeed, Gracie Jane, I will."

Two of the things Tansy loved most: reading and playing the piano. What could be more perfect?

After lunch, which was cold pork and cheese on Ruta's delicious bread and a dish of peach sauce, Tansy was feeling mighty feisty. She had battled the laundry and won, and no one was the wiser.

"Do you know what I'm thinking?" she asked Gracie Jane. When the girl shook her head, Tansy announced, "I think we should go fishing."

CHAPTER 8

*J*esse had stopped by the Pines' cabin and talked with them about Davey coming to the jail and doing odd jobs for him. They were delighted. Davey, however, as much as he admired Jesse, looked skeptical.

"You ain't gonna lock me up for takin' them things, are ya?" he asked Jesse when they were out of earshot of his parents. Jesse just smiled and walked away. Give the lad something to chew on.

On his way back to the jail, he heard commotion down by the river. Then he heard a throaty, bold laugh followed by a familiar childlike squeal. He raced toward the sound, leaping over brush and willows until he came to the river's edge, his heart pounding.

The sight before him stopped him cold. That damn woman would never follow the rules. But there she was with his treasured daughter, who was in her wheelchair, with a fishing pole in her hands!

"You've got a bite!" The widow's voice rang with excitement.

Gracie Jane squealed again, a sound of pure joy, and gently tugged on the pole, the line pulling straight. The fish, if one could call it that, flopped on top of the water. "What do I do?"

The Widow Leigh took the pole, held it high and examined the catch. "Well, honey, it isn't big enough to eat. Why don't we let it go back in the water?" At Gracie Jane's nod, the woman

64

carefully extricated the fish like it was something she did every day and slipped it back into the river.

Jesse pulled in his annoyance, took a deep breath, and exhaled. "What's going on here?" His voice was as tempered as he could make it, considering the circumstances.

"Papa! Papa! I caught a fish. Did you see?" His daughter's eyes sparkled with excitement, her cheeks were rosy, and her smile melted his heart.

"I saw it, sweetheart." His glance landed sternly on the widow. She, too, had a look of pleasure about her, but he thought he saw an underlying look of satisfaction. "How did all of this come about?"

Gracie Jane answered, "Will and Walt and Zeb carried me in my chair to the river, Papa! They picked me up and just carried me right here! Isn't that wonderful?"

His look was still on the widow, and he kept it firm. "They did, did they? And whose idea was this anyway?"

The widow stepped up. "It was mine, of course. Did you think I wouldn't own up to it?"

Jesse combed his fingers through his hair. "Nothing I've said has sunk into that pretty head of yours, has it?"

She took a step back. "'Pretty?'"

Puzzled he said, "What?"

"Did you just call me pretty?" She seemed a bit smug about that too.

"I didn't—I mean, I really—" Had he really said that? He felt himself flush and started to sweat.

She laughed that deep, throaty laugh again, and he blushed further.

"Don't worry, Sheriff, it will be our little secret." She put two fingers between her lips and whistled, and as if on cue, Will and Walt came up over the hill and down to the river, lifted Gracie Jane and her wheelchair, and took her back to the house.

Later, as he mulled over the scene, he continued to think about the widow. She was mysterious, at least to him. Maybe no one else had given her story much thought, but it was his job to find the truth. Even if it meant digging deeper than others, that's what he would do.

At this point, although she claimed to be a farmer's widow, he found no plausible evidence for it. Oh, she looked capable of doing much of what a farm wife would do. The women in his family had all been farm or ranch wives. But their hands were rough and red from washing clothes, washing floors, scouring pans, cleaning stables, feeding chickens, milking goats... The widow's hands were soft and fine looking, as if she'd never done a bit of hard work in her life.

And she was accomplished. He imagined farmer's wives could be, of course, but her skills went beyond that. What farmer's wife has the time to swim, for god's sake? And in his mind, fishing was a man's chore, if one could call it work. Sadly, he didn't ever remember his own mother relaxing, either at the river or anywhere else. And the widow didn't even claim to have children. Most farmers and ranchers he knew relied on family to run a business. That meant offspring, hopefully boys.

She was no debutante. He knew that. She was nothing like Judith. And according to his ex-wife, all society girls were groomed with special skills that would prepare them to run large, expensive households. They weren't taught to swim or fish or hunt or whatever else the widow was adept at doing. Nope, her story didn't add up, at least not to him. His last conversation with Ruta had been frustrating.

"Why are ye being so stubborn about her, Jesse? Why would she lie about who she is?"

"I can't put my finger on it, Ruta. It's a puzzle I intend to solve. If I don't, it'll drive me crazy."

"Well, if ye ask me, which ye didn't, I'd say you're thinking of her a lot for someone ye don't seem to like much."

Was he? Hell, probably. But it wasn't because he was attracted to her. No, it was because in every way possible, she drove him crazy. And he also was a man who needed to solve a mystery.

In the meantime, he found himself comparing her to Judith. Judith was small and dainty and very blond. The widow was tall, had an ample bosom and nearly black hair that curled into masses of ringlets. Judith knew how to flirt. He found that out the hard way, and he still cursed himself for his weakness. The widow didn't look like she knew how, or if she did, wasn't interested in trying her wiles out on him, which was just fine. Judith tittered when she laughed, her dainty hand over her mouth. The widow often threw her head back and guffawed.

Before he went to bed, he could hear her playing the piano, drumming away, and singing along with the men.

"'Camptown racetrack five-mile-long, oh, doo dah day.'"

One morning as Tansy ate breakfast, hotcakes with syrup and berries, she found Ruta studying her. "Do I have something between my teeth?"

Ruta chuckled and sat down across from her, but her hands were always busy. This morning she was cutting up wild rhubarb for sauce. "Ye don't have to worry about the laundry for a while."

How about never? "Oh? Why is that?"

"Louisa and her beau run off and got married. Now she needs the job more than ever." She tipped an apron-full of rhubarb into a bowl in front of her. "Ye'd never done laundry before, have ye?"

Her tone wasn't accusatory, but it put Tansy on alert. "Did I do something wrong?"

Surprising Tansy, Ruta reached across the table and took one of her hands. She turned it over and then back again. "Ye aren't a farmer's wife, are ye? Yer hands are as soft as Gracie Jane's."

Tansy pulled her hand away and tucked it in her lap. She thought about offering up another lie, but she'd done so much of that already, she wasn't sure she could keep track of it. "No, I'm not."

Ruta cocked her head. "Trying to figure ye out is driving Jesse crazy."

Tansy straightened, a little angry. "Why should it bother him who I am?"

"Because he's the sheriff, honey, and it's his job to know what's going on in his town."

"Even if I'm minding my own business?"

At that Ruta laughed. "Ye be minding *his* business—Gracie Jane."

"But I'm doing nothing that will harm her. Even he should be able to see how healthy she looks since we've spent time outdoors."

"He's a might stubborn, I'll give ye that. I think he's softening toward the idea of her having a bit more freedom. 'Tis just hard for him to admit it."

"I think I do frustrate and fluster him sometimes." Tansy leaned across the table. "I promised I wouldn't tell anyone, but the other day he accidently called me 'pretty' and was his face red."

Ruta studied her again. "But ye are pretty."

Tansy blushed. "Oh, you don't have to say that. My mama—"

"Yer mama called ye pretty?"

"Only after she chastised me for being all the things a young woman shouldn't be." She gave Ruta a wan smile.

Ruta pushed the bowl of raw rhubarb aside and put her elbows on the table. "What didn't she think ye should be?"

"Oh, big and tall, loud and outspoken, things like that." Tansy didn't tell her that at one point her mother had told her she was her greatest disappointment. The comment may have hurt her more if she hadn't already known she often frustrated her mother to tears.

"Is that why ye didn't return to your home after yer man died? Because ye and yer mama didn't get on?"

She paused a moment and then said, "There were a lot of reasons I left, Ruta. Mama wasn't the biggest one."

The clock in the foyer struck nine, and Tansy left the table, bringing her dirty dishes to the sink. It was time for Gracie Jane's piano lesson. She left quietly, leaving Ruta to ponder her last remark.

CHAPTER 9

*O*liver tapped the letter on his desk. It was from a jeweler in Topeka, informing him that he had in his possession a Waltham pocket watch with a serial number that indicated the watch had been purchased by Ernest Jarvis in October of 1860.

Oliver's late father-in-law. Oliver had been courting Anastasia for almost a year before the old man died. He remembered the watch, but when had he seen it last? Of course, they hadn't found it in Anastasia's jewelry box. If it had been readily available, she would have pinned it to her blouse and worn it daily, so enamored she was of her pompous father.

Had it been stolen? It was certainly possible, but by whom? And when? And why was it now in the hands of a jeweler in Topeka of all places? He opened his desk drawer and lifted out a piece of his personalized stationary. There was only one way to find out.

Later, at dinner with Grace, he raised the subject of the watch.

She frowned. "Oh, that old thing." She thought a moment, and then added, "I haven't seen that since Ernest died."

"Did you keep it in with your jewelry?"

"I don't think so. Like all of his belongings, once he was gone, I packed things up and stored them away."

"When did you last see it?"

"Like I said, Oliver, I haven't seen it, but then I haven't been looking for it either." She paused, and then asked, "Why are you interested in it now?"

Having decided to keep the letter to himself for the time being, he waved off her question. "Just something I was thinking about, that's all."

"I suppose it should have gone to you," she said quietly, picking at her dessert.

Oliver gave her a gracious smile. "I never wanted that old thing either." But he continued to wonder how the damned watch got as far away as Kansas.

So far, his life without Anastasia was comfortable. He still bore the title of 'that poor widower,' and he liked it. He could dine when he chose and with whom. He could treat clients to dinner without fearing his wife would embarrass him. The only thing he missed was slapping her around after each blunder. Had the old bastard, Ernest, lived, Oliver's life would have been very different. As it was, it had been perfect. But he still wasn't ready to move on. Anastasia's inheritance was now his. He couldn't screw things up.

To tie up one loose end, he had searched for Anastasia's maid and found her working at a large house three streets away. He smothered a grin. She had been terrified when she saw him and learned that he wanted to talk to her. He had watched her carefully as he grilled her, and there was nothing in her demeanor that suggested she was lying or that she knew anything at all. Of course, she had always cowered around him. And she couldn't have taken the jewelry, because she was still here. And the jewelry was gone.

Jesse reread the letter from Emmeline. Maybelle was doing well, Emmeline wrote, but they both missed their little Gracie Jane. If it was at all possible, could he bring her up for a few days?

Their cabin was on the Little Sur River, a sparkling, bubbling stream that held the most generous amounts of rainbow trout in

California. A paradise for a fisherman. He bounded up the steps of the boarding house. By chance he met the widow in the foyer. She wore a blue two-piece dress; the skirt was hemmed with some kind of fancy ribbon. The fabric was so vibrant it brought out the blueness of her eyes. Once again, he quietly cursed himself for lingering on her qualities.

"I have a proposition for you."

She raised a wary eyebrow. She had a pretty face, he had to admit. The dainty cleft in her chin and her masses of nearly black curls gave her an exotic look. Sort of like a gypsy. "And that would be what?"

He explained the situation to her, inviting her along to help with Gracie Jane.

She stepped back, genuinely surprised, and pleased. "That would be wonderful. Is it near the ocean?"

He nodded. "Very close."

She twirled, sending her skirt swishing along the floor. "Oh, Papa told me about the ocean!"

He frowned. "Your pa? I thought your late husband had."

She blinked briefly and then waved away his comment. "My papa as well. Both of them had been in California. When do we leave?"

"As soon as possible. I want to get there before dark." He paused by the door, processing her last remark. "Would you mind packing Gracie Jane's things? I'll get the carryall ready."

Jesse paid close attention to the widow during the ride to the cabin. She held her hand on her hat and strained to see the tops of the redwoods, uttering words of disbelief and excitement.

"It's the tallest tree on earth," he told her.

She gave him a quick glance. "Really? How tall do they get?"

"Some are over three hundred and fifty feet tall and can be as much as fifteen feet in diameter."

She studied them. "That's impressive. They must be very old."

"Some can live two thousand years," he told her. "But as tall as they are, there is another tree that's shorter but larger in diameter. It's the Sequoia. Most of them are further north."

She finally took off her bothersome hat. "My papa told me about them, but I had no idea they were such giants."

Jesse was concerned about the trees, for he'd heard what he hoped were rumors about loggers wanting to come in and help themselves. He didn't mention how upset that made him, or how frustrated he was not to be able to do something about it. The government had structured a new program called the United States Forest Service, but Jesse had no idea how one got involved in such things. And anyway, he wasn't in a position to travel for his job. Not with Gracie Jane to care for.

She gazed at the giants. "What a shame to kill such a beautiful thing."

"Not too far from here is a redwood stump that's so big, I could put the carryall, the horse and everyone in it on top of it with room to spare."

She shook her head slowly, her expression bemused. "I had no idea…"

As if on cue an eagle soared overhead. It appeared to stop midair, then found an air stream and eventually swooped down into the trees. The mourning doves lamented from the brush. But as vast as the forest was, it was still eerily quiet.

"Oh," she exclaimed, "what enormous nests!" She was looking high into the trees where, indeed, there appeared to be a nest.

"That's mistletoe," he answered.

She turned and gave him a curious look. "Really?"

"It grows like that. It's actually a parasite…feeds off the nutrients of the tree."

She made a face and fingered the felt brim of her hat which she kept in her lap. "A parasite. That doesn't sound very festive."

He smiled at her comment. "I guess most people don't know that it sucks the life out of its host."

Later, as she and Gracie Jane sat at the table outside on the grass, the widow appeared totally at ease with his aunts. Their big dog, Bear, nuzzled Gracie Jane as if welcoming her back to the cabin.

"I've never seen such a big dog," the widow exclaimed. "We didn't have pets at home," she added, looking somewhat reticently at the animal.

Jesse said, "I thought all farms had dogs."

"Well...well yes, but they were always outside. In...in the barn," she finished lamely.

All at once a huge raven swooped down and dropped something into Gracie Jane's lap.

The widow, startled, shrieked and leaned toward Gracie Jane, apparently hoping to keep her from harm.

"Don't worry," Gracie Jane said. "It's just Pesky."

The widow settled back into her chair, her hand on her breast. "Pesky?"

Jesse looked over at his daughter's lap. "What has he left for you this time?"

Gracie Jane lifted up a big, round button. "See?"

"The bird left you a button?" The widow was clearly puzzled.

Jesse explained: "Ever since I've been bringing Gracie Jane to the cabin, the raven has deposited a gift of some sort for her."

Emmeline leaned across the table. "Why, look Maybelle, it's that the button from my winter coat!"

Maybelle peered at it over the top of her spectacles. "Indeed, it is. I thought you lost that the day we went shopping in Willow River."

"Well, I did. But I thought it was long gone somewhere in town."

Emmeline looked at the widow. "Now you see why we call him Pesky." She went into the cabin and returned with a covered tin. She handed it to Gracie Jane. "Show her what he's brought you, honey."

Gracie Jane opened the tin and put the lid on the table. She plucked out a feather. "It's an eagle feather," she said proudly. She brought out a number of other gifts, including a coin, a small round shiny stone, what appeared to be a bird's beak, a small pinecone, and a tiny bone.

The widow fingered the stone, rubbing its shiny surface. "Are you telling me this…this bird actually knows who you are?"

"Ravens and crows are very intelligent birds," Jesse offered. He thought about telling her how he had been tracking their behavior, but decided it was probably more than she wanted to know. He glanced at her. She had a strange smile on her face.

"What?"

"I was thinking about Edgar Allan Poe," she answered.

"You mean, 'Quoth the raven, 'nevermore'?"

"Exactly. I love his stories."

"They're kind of depressing, aren't they?" he asked.

She settled back in her chair and gazed into the cloudless sky. "Yes, I know. But I guess there's a side to me that enjoys it."

He watched her for a moment, and then said, "So the widow has a dark side?"

She stopped smiling and suddenly appeared sad. "I guess so. Something like that."

Things were quiet for a spell, and then Emmeline said something about the weather.

The widow exclaimed, "Oh, but really. It's lovely and invigorating. You must feel like you're in heaven every day. And the smell of those pine needles." She inhaled sharply and exhaled. "It's an aroma I've never come across before. It's a most intoxicating perfume! We should bottle it. We'd get rich!"

They all laughed. Even Jesse couldn't help himself. The widow's enthusiasm was infectious, and he wished she'd do something stupid so he could stop thinking about her.

Jesse pulled up a chair. "Mrs. Leigh wants to see the ocean."

She turned to him. "Oh, please. Call me Tansy. Everyone does."

Could he?

Maybelle limped out from the cabin with a covered jar which she set on the table. "Guess what I made this morning, Gracie Jane?"

Gracie Jane's eyes got big. "My favorite?"

"Your favorite." She opened the lid and shoved the jar toward Gracie Jane, who leaned forward and plucked out 'her favorite.'

"Honey popcorn balls," she said around a mouthful. "I just love them."

"And I made some Boston molasses bread we'll have with supper," Emmeline said. "Maybe you can catch us some trout, Jesse."

He leaned into his chair, his arms folded across his chest. "I think your guest might like to try her hand at that." He had trouble calling her Tansy. It seemed so intimate.

She sat up straight. "Oh, might I?"

Maybelle studied her, surprised. "You like to fish?"

"Oh, yes. It was one of my favorite times with my papa when I was a young girl." She appeared to get a little misty-eyed. Jesse realized that ever since they left Willow River, her demeanor had slowly changed. They were no longer at odds with one another.

Emmeline got up from the table. "Well, you can't fish in those clothes, now can you?"

Tansy glanced at her travel suit. "I really didn't bring that much with me."

"Not to worry," Emmeline said. "Come inside with me. I'll get you fixed up if you don't mind wearing someone else's clothes."

"As long as they're comfortable for fishing, that's all I care about."

They went inside, and a short while later the widow came out wearing Emmeline's Hodgman waders. She also wore a pair of twill trousers and a shirt that Jesse knew belonged to Maybelle. Despite the fact that in his mind she looked rather silly, she appeared to be ecstatic over the change in her wardrobe. Judith wouldn't have been caught dead in anything but her fashionable gowns and corsets no matter how uncomfortable they may have been. And of course, she stuck her nose in the air when it came to doing something like handling a fish.

He had to wonder why he was forever comparing the two women.

Emmeline fetched the fishing pole. "I'll show you the best

spot." They left, Emmeline in the lead and the widow, quite agile despite the waders, kept pace. Bear lumbered along behind.

"Papa, I want to see the river, too."

"I do too," he answered. "Why don't I just pick you up and carry you down there?"

Gracie Jane nodded and lifted her arms toward him. He plucked her from the wheelchair as if she weighed no more than a feather. She put an arm around his neck and snuggled in. She still had a baby smell about her. He inhaled deeply.

"Oh, Papa, I do so love it here."

Jesse did too. If he didn't have to make a living, he would come here much more often. Maybe even build a place of his own. He was handy that way. When he was a boy, he'd built a tree house all by himself. It still existed somewhere in the woods. He wondered if he could find it. Hell, wouldn't that be something if he could make a living out here? He could dream, couldn't he?

They sat on a fallen log and watched the widow fish.

"She's really good at it, isn't she, Papa?"

He had to agree. She appeared at ease in trousers and fishing waders. She tossed a line like a man. But she wasn't a man. She was a woman like none other he had ever known. She had curves and flesh where it should be (the picture of her in her swimming attire never left his brain) and compassion. She took to his daughter without batting an eye. But he wasn't interested. No, he'd gone down that path once before, and he wasn't going there again. But he did wonder what it would be like to do so...

For supper they had trout, potatoes fried with onions and greens from a small garden near the cabin. The fresh air was so invigorating, Tansy was starving when they sat down outside at the table. "The trout is wonderful, even if I do say so myself. I really love the way you fixed it."

Maybelle smiled. "Yes, indeed. And I surely thank you for

skinning it and taking out those bones. You did a mighty nice job."

She knew the sheriff watched her when she cleaned the trout. It didn't bother her. Papa always said if you catch a fish for supper, you'd better know how to clean it.

Tansy savored each bite, trying not to bolt down her food and look like an animal, as her mama would say. Or Oliver. She pushed away thoughts of him. He alone could spoil her appetite. She gazed at the scene around her. The sky was so blue it almost hurt her eyes, and the scent of the pines, heavy and succulent, wafted in the air. Pinecones were strewn about, and an occasional squirrel scooted by, dashing up one tree, deftly making its way to another.

"Tell me about the land," she said, glancing around her.

"Our roots go back generations," Jesse began. "First, by the natives, the Esselen tribe and then, after the Spanish came, we learned there had been comingling."

"Comingling?"

"I suppose you could call it marriage of sorts. But we are clearly a mix of Esselen, Spanish and some white mountain men who roamed the area."

Tansy listened, transfixed. "That is so exciting. Where I'm from, everyone is pretty much the same. Blue eyes, blond hair, pale skin, and the list goes on. Except for me, of course, and I stuck out like a camel on an iceberg."

"Where did you grow up?" Emmeline asked, leaning forward.

Tansy paused a moment. She was tired of trying to keep track of her fabrications. "Illinois. Near Chicago," she answered.

"I hear tell they've got a pretty lake up that way," Maybelline said.

"Lake Michigan. Yes, it's quite pretty. But it's always cold."

Both women nodded. "Jesse told us you're a widow. It must be hard for you to be on your own."

Tansy stood and began clearing the table. "I'm no worse off than most women in my predicament. Now," she added, hoping to change the subject, "lead me to the kitchen so we can get these dishes cleaned up."

She did notice that Jesse and his aunts gave each other puzzled glances.

Later, after the sun slid behind the rugged mountain walls, bathing them in hues of lavender, Tansy got Gracie Jane ready for bed. The aunts had prepared an oat paste patch for her skin problem and then wrapped it with another cloth to keep it in place. She was to sleep on a small cot near the fireplace. Once again, as in her room at the rooming house, Tansy noticed the colorful quilts the women brought out from a cupboard.

"Can we read *Little Women*?" Gracie Jane asked.

"Of course." The others went outside, and Tansy brought the kerosene lamp over near the cot. She tucked Gracie Jane in and sat on the bed.

"'As spring came on, a new set of amusements became the fashion...'" Tansy continued reading until she noticed Gracie Jane was asleep. She knew she should go outside to see the others, but the sweet little girl looked so comfortable, Tansy couldn't resist lying down beside her, pulling the child into the cocoon of her body.

———

"So, Jesse," Maybelle began. "Tell us about your widow."

Jesse put his cigarette out in an ashtray on the table. "She's not my widow."

"Oh, you know what I mean," his aunt answered.

Yes, he knew what she meant. So he told them everything, from the moment he thought she was drowning in the river, to the realization she was qualified to tutor Gracie Jane, to the fact that she had said she was a farmer's widow.

"That's what puzzles me," he said.

Emmeline looked up from her knitting. The kerosene lamp between the three of them cast misty shadows over the table. "Why is that?"

"Her hands. I've never met a working woman whose hands weren't rough and calloused and red most of the time."

The aunts nodded, glancing at their own roughened hands.

"But why would she lie about that, Jesse?" Maybelle set the bowl of fresh vegetables from the garden aside and rested her elbows on the table.

He expelled a sigh. "I don't know, but I'd like to find out."

"Well," Maybelle said, "being the sheriff and all, it's your duty to find out those things, I imagine." She searched the table. "I forgot the paring knife. Jesse, will you go inside, and fetch it for me?"

Jesse obliged. He stepped into the cabin, and his gaze went directly to the cot by the fireplace. A small fire burned, and with the kerosene lamp on low, he could clearly see the two figures on the cot.

Something odd lurched in his chest. The widow was curled around Gracie Jane in a protective and loving manner, as if she would shield her from harm. They were both asleep. Gracie Jane's reddish brown hair spread out on the pillow, and the widow's mass of dark ringlets framed her face.

The odd feeling that came over him caused him to stagger, and he grabbed the back of a chair for support.

He couldn't feel this way. He wouldn't allow himself to. After all, she was still a stranger with a mysterious past, one which she seemed reluctant to share. Every scenario possible had already gone through his mind. Not one of them made much sense to him.

She might be pretending to be something she was not, but she couldn't be playacting about her enthusiasm for Big Sur. Tomorrow he would take her over to the ocean. He was anxious to see it himself. The noise, the brisk breeze, the vastness of it always brought him peace. And later tomorrow night, after dark, he'd make another trip over there to check on something else…

He gave the two on the cot one more glance. Not much peace in his soul at the moment, however.

CHAPTER 10

*A*lthough the cabin was close to the coast, the route to get there was rutted and rock filled. As Tansy followed Jesse, who was carrying Gracie Jane in a special sling around his neck, Tansy recalled earlier in the morning when she'd awakened. Something had been touching her nose. She would brush it away, and it would return. Finally, she opened her eyes to find Gracie Jane on her elbow, her other hand holding a tiny feather, and her face wreathed in a big grin.

"Good. You're awake." She glanced toward the room where the aunts slept. "I really have to use the necessary, Miss Tansy."

Tansy squirmed and felt her own discomfort.

After they used the necessary, she noticed Jesse's bedroll rolled up near the carryall. He ambled out from the woods, Bear beside him.

"Did you sleep outdoors?" she asked.

"I did. It's where I always sleep when I'm here."

Suddenly she realized it was foggy, and a wave of disappointment washed over her. He must have read her mind because he assured her, "Fog always creeps in at night. But it will be gone before noon. Don't worry."

And he was right. By noon the fog was gone, and they were on their way. Before she stepped out through the last of the brush and trees, she heard the roar. Now the Pacific Ocean was finally before her. She couldn't move. The only thing she felt was an incredible, overwhelming urge to sob with joy. How to explain it to someone who has not seen it? Impossible. The sky and the ocean went on forever. She had never imagined such beauty and magnificence. She could barely breathe.

"Here." Jesse handed her binoculars. She lifted them to her eyes and squinted through, panning over the vast blue water with the whitecaps that appeared as far as the eye could see. She continued to search the expanse and suddenly, not too far from shore, saw something break through the waves and then slap the surface of the water, sending spray high into the air. She gasped. "A whale! I just saw a whale!"

She turned and glanced at Jesse, who watched her with an odd expression on his face. "Probably a Blue Whale. They're often around here this time of year."

"And I hear barking. Are those sea lions?"

"Sea lions and otters," he added.

In the distance she heard the seagulls scream. It was familiar to her, yet here at the ocean, she thought they sounded excited to be alive, not afraid, as they did at home. *Home.* There it was again. Would it ever truly be home again after seeing this part of the country?

She stumbled toward a flat rock of granite and sat, unable to speak. Unable to move, tears rolling down her cheeks, she didn't reach up to wipe them away.

"Miss Tansy, are you crying?"

Gracie Jane's concern made Tansy smile. "Yes, I guess I am." She wiped her cheeks with the back of her hand.

"But, why? Aren't you happy?"

She looked at the child, still tucked close to her papa's chest. "Gracie Jane, I have never been happier in my entire life."

"You cry when you're happy?"

Tansy dug into her pocket for her handkerchief. "I guess I do. I don't think I've ever been this happy before."

Her father had spoken of the ocean, of course. He had mentioned it, but nothing could compare with actually seeing it. The massive coastline with the huge granite boulders climbing into the skies and the scrubby shrubs and trees that clung perilously to the rocky surface was not something one could explain. Nothing he had told her could have prepared her for the grandeur, the majesty of the California coast. And she was here, taking it all in, wishing so very much that she could share her feelings with her father.

Finally, she found her voice. "I had no idea anything could be so beautiful. It goes beyond beauty. How can someone not believe there's a God when they see this?" She was not a particularly religious person, but for her, religion had nothing to do with her belief in God.

She knew they couldn't stay. The afternoon sun was sinking, and soon it would be dark. She wanted to climb the rocks, stand up high above them, and feel the wind in her hair, blowing her skirts out behind her. Better yet, if she only had her own trousers, she would wear them to climb. What a life people had out here!

Reluctantly she followed Jesse and Gracie Jane back through the brush, toward the rutted path that led to the cabin. She knew in her soul that if she never saw the ocean again, she would carry a picture of it in her heart and her head, leaving nothing, no crashing wave against the granite outcroppings, no soaring eagles and condors, no endless blue sky, no vastness toward the horizon uncharted.

That night Tansy was so excited and happy she couldn't sleep. She slid from the cot, careful not to wake Gracie Jane, and went to the window. She cupped her hands around her eyes to shut out the small light from the fireplace and saw something moving around the carryall. It was Jesse. He seemed to be putting some things together. When he was done, he left, taking the path toward the ocean that they had gone on earlier in the day.

Tansy turned from the window, her gaze falling on the waders she'd worn when she fished for trout. Not giving it too much thought, she pulled them on and crept out of the cabin, intent on learning what Jesse was up to.

Bear lifted his head from his spot by the fireplace but didn't follow her.

Thankfully there was a moon. Tansy wouldn't have had any idea where she was going otherwise. And as quiet as Jesse was, she could hear him up ahead of her. She followed him down a path they hadn't taken before, and the ocean's roar became louder and louder as they descended. He stopped behind a boulder and appeared to be watching the surf.

Tansy didn't see anything, but she crept up behind him and touched his shoulder.

He turned swiftly and grabbed her arm, pulling it behind her back and pinning her against the rock. She winced at the pain but didn't cry out. He got right into her face but suddenly realized who she was.

"Good God," he said, "what in the hell are you doing?"

When he released her, she rubbed her arm and said, "I followed you."

"Well, that's damned obvious, but why?"

She hunkered down beside him behind the boulder. "Because I couldn't sleep, and I saw you moving around. I was curious. What are you doing anyway?"

He muttered something and sighed. "I got word that poachers are after the sea otters. Again."

"And you think they'll come here?"

"Well," he began, a bit testy, "they might have had there not been so much commotion."

She wrinkled her nose. "Sorry."

She felt his hand on her thigh. "What in the devil are you wearing?"

"Emmeline's waders." She heard him chuckle. "Well, I didn't have time to dress and these were handy."

He stood and helped her up. "We aren't going to catch anyone tonight. Might as well go back to the cabin."

Disappointed, she said, "Really? It's so beautiful down here. Can't we stay for a while?" She looked out over the ocean where the moon cast a watery shadow over the tranquil surface.

She felt him study her in the darkness. "All right. But I know a better spot. Follow me."

She followed him to a log that appeared to have been made into a bench. They sat, shoulder to shoulder, and watched and listened to the surf. Of all the music Tansy knew, this was the most beautiful.

Jesse's shoulder was warm against hers, and she felt a strange nudge of pleasure between her thighs. And she liked it.

She had fallen asleep, for when she woke, Bear's nose was in her face. She glanced at the sheriff; he was studying her, a wry smile on his face.

"How long have I been asleep?" She rubbed her eyes and yawned.

He glanced toward the sky. "It's nearly dawn."

She scooted and sat up straight, twinging at an achy muscle. "And you've been sitting there, watching me the whole time?"

He had the grace to look sheepish. "I fell asleep too. Emmeline must have let Bear out early. He probably wondered where we were and came looking for us."

"Do you really think dogs reason?"

He scratched Bear's ears. "I think they know more than we give them credit for."

Tansy stood, ready to return to the cabin, only briefly wondering what a mess she must be, having slept outside, sitting up, in Emmeline's waders.

"Now," she said, rather impishly, "don't tell anyone we slept together." She was kidding, of course, but after she said the words, she felt herself blush.

The next day, Tansy ventured out on her own into the trees, and Bear, who apparently knew his job well, trailed after her, making sure she didn't wander too far from the cabin.

She picked up a huge pinecone that had fallen to the ground. It was woody yet pliable. She studied it, noting how symmetrical and handsome it was, and scooped it into the apron

Emmeline had loaned her. Columbine, pink and yellow, sprouted from the most unimaginable places. A woodpecker… what had the sheriff called it? She smiled and glanced at the lump in her apron. Acorn woodpecker, he had said, hammered away at a tree nearby. There was birdsong. She heard skittering movement in the leaves and pine needles that covered the forest floor, imagining voles and mice and squirrels, oblivious to her silent presence. And Bear knew too, as he stood as still as a statue beside her.

But all of a sudden, he growled low in this throat. Tansy saw that the hair on his neck and back stood on end. Swallowing hard, she tried not to move as she followed Bear's gaze. There! Her heart jumped into her throat. There, barely visible on a slab of rock behind a screen of trees, was…something. She didn't know what. Mountain lion? Bobcat? Except for the pounding of her heart, she was motionless.

She dared not breathe until a movement in the trees must have indicated to the dog that all was clear, for he snuffled against her skirt. She reached down and scratched the dog's ears. "We don't have to mention this to the sheriff now, do we?" They returned to the cabin, but all the way Tansy's heart thumped loudly in her chest. But oh, how she loved the excitement!

That afternoon, the sheriff approached her. "I built a tree house around here somewhere when I was a boy. I'm going to go on a hunt for it. Want to join me?"

"Oh, that sounds like fun." She followed him into the woods, happy to be behind him so she could study him. He was tall, quite a bit taller than she was. His shoulders were wide, pulling the denim of his shirt tightly across his back and his hair, a bit long, curled against his collar.

His hips were narrow, and he looked very fine indeed in his denim jeans. She had noticed that from the front, he filled them out very nicely behind the buttons of his fly. He seemed so amiable now that they were away from his work.

He stopped in front of her and pointed. "There."

Tansy followed his gaze and saw it. It had a floor, four walls, and a roof of sorts. There was even a tiny window cut into the side facing the ocean, although she was certain a person couldn't see it from up there. "Is it sturdy?"

"We'll just have to find out, won't we?" He strode to the tree, found his footing, and climbed it, agile as a boy. When he got to the top, he stood, his hand shielding his eyes from the sun, and stared beyond the treetops.

From the bottom, Tansy asked, "What do you see?"

He shook his head and stared. "I don't remember being able to see the ocean before."

Excited, she said, "You can see the ocean from up there? I'm coming up."

"Wait," he called. "I'm not sure it's safe."

"Oh, pooh. If you can do it, so can I."

"In a dress?"

She gave him a glance that clearly said, 'just watch me.' "I was climbing trees before I learned to swim." And with that, she hiked up her skirt, went to the tree, and discovered there were little steps nailed into the trunk. She was up beside him in a matter of seconds. And when she followed his gaze, her breath caught in her throat. Indeed, she could see the ocean. A vast blue painting on the horizon, speckled with sparkling crystals where the sun bounced off the waves. In the opposite direction stood the granite peaks of the mountain range. "The mountains are very masculine."

He gave her a curious look. "In what way?"

"They're rugged and unyielding. I don't sense any softness."

"They're a mixture of granite, marble, sandstone, limestone… and yeah, I guess you're right. Pretty formidable."

"How is it that you know what they're made of?"

With a shrug, he said, "It's kind of a pastime of mine." He studied them for a long moment and then added, "I do love these mountains, but I don't trust them."

"That's an odd way to put it."

"No, really," he said. "They're like a big, wild animal you wouldn't turn your back on. I feel that way mostly in the winter. Storms up here are notorious for raising havoc."

He stood behind her, close enough so she could feel his

warmth. His breath rustled the hair at her ear. She could turn just slightly and find his face close to hers…

She cleared her throat. "What's the closest town?"

He pointed south. "San Simeon. It was a Spanish mission."

She nodded. "Of course. Saint Simon. One who hears and listens." She glanced behind her. "Do the mountains have a name?"

"Santa Lucia."

"Saint Lucy," she translated. "I read about her when I was just a girl. She came from wealth but was forced to marry…" Tansy thought of her own situation. "And when her husband discovered she wanted to give her wealth to the poor, he made sure she suffered for it."

"How?" Jesse asked.

Tansy dug her toe into a knothole in the floor board. "First they sent her to a brothel. After that, they tried to drag her away, but they couldn't move her. When they couldn't move her, they lit a fire under her to burn her. When that didn't work, they finally killed her with a sword."

"Tough to be a martyr."

"Yes," she answered. "And things aren't all that different today."

"I don't think we burn people at the stake anymore," he suggested.

"Sometimes I think they would if they could."

"Who?"

She paused a moment, and then said, "Husbands."

Both were quiet for a long while, allowing the surroundings to envelop them.

"I could stay up here forever," she said, the sight before her hypnotic.

"A little tough to do without the proper facilities," he said, his voice holding a smile.

She breathed in the pungent, earthy air. "I suppose there is that. But how idyllic it would be to live out here and be able to see the ocean anytime I wanted." She turned and found him watching her, his eyes surprisingly warm. Another tingle settled low in her belly. "Thank you for sharing this."

He cocked a grin. "The treehouse?"

"Everything. From the minute we got here until the time we have to leave, it's been, well, one of the most perfect times of my life," she admitted.

"You must have led quite a sheltered life," he murmured as he prepared to climb down.

No, not sheltered, she thought, merely boring and after her papa died, unhappy.

The night before they were to leave, she returned from the necessary and saw Jesse leaning against the carryall, studying the sky.

She stopped and looked up as well. The air was so clear the sky looked like a blanket of tiny blinking lights.

She joined him. Their silence was comfortable until Jesse spoke. "When I was a boy, I heard the story of the Dark Watchers."

She tucked a stray curl behind her ear. "What are they?"

"Giant human-like specters that are seen at twilight, silhouetted against the night sky."

"You mean, like people?"

"In a way. But when you see one, you're sure it's real until it suddenly vanishes like a wisp of smoke."

"Big Sur lore, I gather," she mused. "Have you ever seen one?"

"Yes, once. It was up ahead of me. I called, asking who he was, for it looked like a human shape to me. It up and disappeared."

She lifted her shoulders and shuddered. "Very eerie."

They sat in silence again, until he asked, "You're not a farmer's widow, are you?"

She couldn't pretend anymore. "What gave you that idea?"

He shifted, crossing his arms over his chest. "Your hands."

"So you've apparently discussed this with Ruta."

"No," he was quick to say, "I mentioned it to her, but she didn't think it meant anything."

Tansy recalled the moment Ruta had asked her the same question.

"And there were other things," he continued.

"Such as?"

He turned and looked at her, the moon glancing off his face, illuminating his eyes. "You see how my aunts work. My ma worked the same way. There was no time for fun. There was always something to do. They lived near the ocean but never learned to swim. There wasn't time for that. They could hunt if they had to, but usually that was a man's job."

"And fishing?" she added, hoping not to sound sarcastic.

His gave her a half smile. "Where I grew up, that was a man's job, too."

She felt a little aggressive. "So you're saying that because my hands are soft, I haven't been exposed to heavy work. What if I used gloves?"

"Did you?"

She glanced away. "No."

"Before the other day, had you ever done laundry?"

She flushed and shook her head.

He touched her jaw, and she automatically flinched and stepped away, a reflex from her not so distant past.

She could see the wheels turning in his head. "Just who are you, Tansy Leigh?"

She couldn't form an answer. All she could do was fold her arms across her stomach and hurry into the cabin.

There was a bit of a kerfuffle when they returned to Willow River. Jesse dropped the others at the rooming house and went straight to the jail where Lloyd was pacing back and forth, wearing a path in the floor boards.

On seeing Jesse, his whole demeanor changed. "Oh, thank god you're back." He was sweating.

Jesse tossed his hat on the peg by the door. "What's the problem?"

Lloyd did look a bit bedraggled. His hair looked like a bird had nested in it, and his clothes were wrinkled. "It's them Pines!"

Jesse expelled a sigh and rubbed his forehead. "What now?"

"Jesse," Lloyd began, "I tried to break it up. I really did. I did like you always do. I waited for them to see me and then expected them to be all nice like."

"And?"

"And it didn't happen! They continued screaming and cussing each other out. I had to wrestle a skillet from Margot, or she'd have slung it across the room at Bert's head."

Jesse ran his fingers through his hair. "So then what happened?"

Lloyd glanced toward the back room where the cells were. "They're back there."

Jesse couldn't suppress a laugh. "You put them in jail?"

"I didn't know how else to stop them, Jesse. They just wouldn't quit going at each other, and I was afraid they'd hurt someone, especially Davey. Or me," he added, a bit sheepishly.

"So let me get this straight. Margot and Bert are in jail, and Davey is left at home by himself."

Lloyd stepped nervously from one foot to the other. "Well, yeah, but it's only been since early this morning."

"Did you separate them back there?"

Lloyd flushed and scratched his scraggly mass of hair. "Didn't think to."

With a shake of his head, Jesse went into the back room, grabbing the keys off the hook by the door. They were still at it. He could hear them long before he saw them. Lloyd had put them in the farthest cell from the door.

The minute he came into view, Margot and Bert stopped squabbling, and each gave him a big, warm smile. "Well, morning, Sheriff. Where've you been? We missed you."

Jesse hooked his thumbs in his pockets and studied them. He

doubted they would have an answer for him if he asked why their behaviors changed every time he walked into a room.

He opened the cell door and flung it wide. "You're free to go. And when you get home, send Davey to see me."

"He isn't in trouble, is he?" Margot's face was lined with worry.

"No. I just have a little work for him to do."

Both of them smiled. "Well, thanks again, Sheriff, and tell that Lloyd fellow we don't hold any grudges."

Jesse gave them a dismissive wave and watched them walk away, Bert's arm around his wife's shoulders.

When he was alone in the office, he sat back in his chair and thought about the widow Leigh. Or was she a widow? Her refusal to answer his question about who she was nagged him still.

He'd decided she definitely was running from something, but she didn't seem like the type of woman who would be in trouble with the law. But there were all kinds, weren't there?

Last night after everyone was asleep, he thought about her and had to squelch a laugh. He imagined her creeping down the path to the beach in Em's waders. And she'd scared the hell out of him when she touched him. Christ, it could have been the poachers. More specifically, it could have been Lester and his gang of hoodlums. That's who he'd been waiting for.

He wanted to return to the cabin, but she'd insisted on staying. Something about her was fragile, he knew, for she saw things that most women he knew wouldn't even notice.

And after she'd fallen asleep against his shoulder, he looked at her, her dark, thick eyelashes brushing her cheeks, her luscious mouth slightly open as she breathed, and he wondered for the umpteenth time, who she really was. And why she, of all women, had begun to dig a path toward his heart.

He shook himself. If he ever caught that bunch clubbing sea otters to death again, he'd grab one and use it on them. That was a promise he had made to himself. It was bad enough that there were still whalers out there killing the blues, the orcas, and the humpbacks. There wasn't much he could do about that by himself. But if he could save a few otters and seals, it might give him a little peace.

The door opened, and Davey poked his head in. "You wanted to see me, Sheriff?"

Jesse motioned him in and to a chair beside the desk. "It seems we have a little problem, don't we, Davey?"

Davey studied his ragged fingernails and chewed on his lip. "I ain't no thief, Sheriff."

"What would you call it?"

Davey shrugged. "What I took didn't seem to belong to anyone. I never saw anyone around."

"You didn't see the woman swimming in the river when you took her cape?"

His head came up. "How'd you know I took it?"

"Because your ma was wearing it a while back, and she said you'd given it to her."

Realizing he'd been found out, Davey explained, "I kept it for a while, thinking someone would ask about it, but no one ever did." He shrugged again. "Thought my ma should have something fine when winter comes along."

"Why didn't you bring it here?"

"Dunno. Guess I didn't think of it."

"Did you enjoy Ruta's pie?"

His face flushed, and he bit back a smile. "It was darn good. Ate it all myself and didn't even get a belly ache."

Jesse went to a small closet where he took out a broom. "Until school starts, I want you to come in here every afternoon and sweep out the cells. I'll have other small jobs for you to do as well. Can you handle it?"

"Are you punishing me?"

Jesse gave the boy a lopsided smile. "Would you rather I lock you up for stealing?"

He returned the grin. "Lloyd locked up my ma and pa."

Jesse really hadn't known the Pines all that long. They had moved into the cabin by the river a year ago. "Do they always fight, Davey?"

"That ain't fighting," he reasoned.

"What would you call it?" Jesse asked, perplexed.

"It's just the way they are."

"Then why do you ask me to come and break them up?"

"'Cuz they like to see you," Davey answered, as if it was obvious.

Jesse sat on the edge of his desk and studied the boy. He was bright, inquisitive, quick to learn and never appeared bruised or hurt in any way. At least Margot and Bert abused each other and not Davey.

He shoved the broom at him. "Get those cells swept out."

Davey hopped up, took the broom, and disappeared into the back room.

Tansy dusted the piano, cleaned the keys, and closed the lid. There was a layer of dust on the table next to the settee, so she wiped that up as well. She felt a bit guilty about how she handled the situation with the sheriff the last night at the cabin. And to be honest with herself, she realized that holding everything in was giving her heartburn or indigestion or something because her stomach burned.

Often at night, when she couldn't fall asleep, she thought about her family back home. She wondered if Oliver missed her or was happy to be rid of her. As a 'widower' he still had her money, so Tansy was quite certain he wasn't missing her at all. Of course, there was no proof she was actually dead. Didn't they need a body for that? Therefore, Oliver was probably gnashing his teeth over that little problem. And Mother? Oh, yes, Mama would miss her, if only because she would have no one else to nag.

That was unfair. Perhaps Tansy hoped her mother wouldn't miss her too much, just to stave off her own sense of guilt.

Had she left any loose ends? She thought about that quite a lot. But nothing came back to haunt her. She had been careful in every respect. But what if she had somehow slipped up? That thought brought another burning pain to her stomach.

She couldn't keep everything inside much longer, or she'd be visiting the local doctor for something to coat her stomach. Obviously Ruta's whiskey laced coffee didn't do the trick.

She heard Jesse's voice in the kitchen. When she arrived, he sat nursing the toxic coffee.

"Sheriff," she began, drawing in a sigh, "We have to talk."

CHAPTER 11

$\mathscr{A}$fter Oliver had reread the letter, he'd gone completely still. His heart rammed his ribs, and he thought something in his head might explode. The response to his letter from the Topeka jeweler shocked and bewildered him. He read it a third time:

Dear Mr. Radcliffe,

In response to your questions about the Waltham watch, I can only tell you the following: My associate, who has since died, waited on the customer and listed the items she wanted to sell.

She?

Here is a list:

1. Waltham pocket watch (of which you are aware).
2. One pair gold drop earrings with diamonds and rubies.
3. Gold bangle bracelet with circle of diamonds.
4. Three carat cushion cut diamond ring.
5. A sterling silver bangle bracelet with fancy lapped serpentine ends.

The remainder of the letter wasn't important. Oliver didn't even care how much she had gotten for the jewelry. Now he sat behind his desk, the letter forgotten as thoughts whirled and spun and whipped around in his head. He picked up the exquisitely carved onyx owl he used as a paper weight and hefted it in his palm.

Comprehension began to sink in, a thought that never in a million years would have occurred to him had this not come about. It simmered and seethed, wrapping around his consciousness like a snake, squeezing venom into his bloodstream which, in turn, became deadly wrath.

The night she drowned, she claimed to not be ready and told him to go on ahead. That should have been a clue because she was always punctual. And wearing all of that jewelry had been gaudy at best, and if anything, she rarely wore any of it. Had this been her plan all along?

But how was it possible? Why would she do it? His rage erupted, and he hefted the onyx owl across the room where it hit a painting of Lake Michigan and shattered the glass, sending shards everywhere.

Ellis Crawford left his new client's office and headed to his favorite watering hole to go over his notes. He didn't much care for the wealthy sons-of-bitches who called for his skills, but they had the money. He'd been a private dick for ten years and loved his job. No wife, no kids, no responsibility to anyone but himself. Not having to share the money was pretty damned good too.

He settled himself into a back booth and waved at the bartender. While he waited for his beer, he looked over his notes. Wife gone missing. Presumed drowned in boating accident in late May. He noted the date. Jewelry sold to jeweler in Topeka—by a woman. He noted the date there as well.

He'd have to check the train schedule. But had she stayed in Topeka or gone on further? He had his work cut out for him, but he felt invigorated. Damn but he loved his job! He got to chase women, and when he caught them, he didn't even have to keep them.

Oliver paced his study. The new maid had come in and cleaned up the glass just before the detective arrived, but Oliver saw pieces of glass everywhere he looked. Or maybe it was because he wanted to break everything else in sight. But he knew nothing would lessen his rage.

Now, two days later, his thoughts went again to Anastasia's maid, Clarice, the one he'd let go. Could they have planned this together? But no. He had already grilled her and was certain she knew nothing.

Grace opened the study door and rapped a few times just to let him know she was there. She knew nothing of this. So far, he had kept it to himself. But if his wife was alive, her mother should know about it. For all of her failings, Grace was a decent person. For Anastasia to have pulled this trick on her family was unconscionable.

"Sit down, Grace."

She raised her eyebrows, surprised at his tone. "Is something wrong?"

He poured her a glass of sherry, which she took with another expression of surprise. "Sherry? At this hour?"

He poured himself a whiskey and sat down beside her. "I have to tell you something I've discovered."

He gave her the first letter from the jeweler in Topeka, which she read, growing increasingly perplexed. "Ernest's watch was in Kansas?" She brought the letter down hard on her lap, her eyes narrowing in anger. "So one of the servants did steal it."

"I wrote back for more information." He drew the second missive from his inside pocket and handed it to her. With the same bewilderment, she began to read. When she finished, she looked at him and shook her head, the crepe-like wattle of skin on her neck swaying back and forth.

"I don't understand."

Oliver took a large gulp of his drink and then stood and paced the room. "I'm glad you're sitting down, Grace, because I think Anastasia is alive."

The glass of sherry tumbled to the floor, spilling out onto the carpet. "What?"

He stopped and looked at her. She was studying him, a dangerous look in her eyes. "That's the most preposterous thing I've ever heard."

He motioned to the letter. "Read it again—"

"I don't have to," she interrupted. "Whatever made you say such a thing?" Now she was getting weepy.

He sat beside her again and took her hands in his. "Grace, the jeweler listed the items that the woman sold. The diamond, the earrings, and the bracelets were described perfectly. And the watch had a number on it, which came back as belonging to Ernest."

"Oh, Oliver, as much as I'd like to believe you, it can't be true. My God, I hate to think of it, but maybe she…her body washed up on shore and someone took the items from her." She put her face in her hands and wept.

He hadn't thought of that. Was he so anxious to believe she was alive? Why? So he could bring her home and punish her for what she'd done to him? It would have to be very special punishment. No one dupes him and gets away with it.

"Grace." His voice was condescending. "Would you prefer to believe she's dead? Even if we have a slim chance of knowing who this mystery woman is who sold the jewelry, wouldn't you rather it be Anastasia?"

Grace's head came up with a snap. "Why? To find out she'd rather live anywhere but with those who love her? To learn that she's put all of us, including her sister and my granddaughters, through absolute hell? And if it's true, what will everyone think? My god, they would probably think she'd gone crazy to pull such a stunt."

"I know it doesn't sound sane or sensible. Perhaps…perhaps she did have some kind of hysterical moment. She did act strangely toward the end, don't you remember?" Was he planting a seed? Perhaps…

Grace expelled a shaky sigh. "Well, I do recall that she was late that night. Remember? She was never late. Never."

He scrubbed his hand over his chin. "And I remember one night she didn't come to bed, and when I went looking for her, she was standing at the window in my den, just staring out into the night." This was true. He hadn't put any stock in it before, but now, now he could use it and other oddities against her. *When* he found her.

The plan that formed in his mind almost made him smile, but he stayed stoic. "Do you remember anything else, Grace?"

She pinched her eyebrows together, appearing to search her brain, unwittingly to give him more ammunition. She looked up, sharply. "One day when you were gone and I was here, she was actually folding laundry!"

"Quite out of character for a lady, don't you think?"

"Well, of course. We have servants for that. And she always wanted to dress herself and do her own hair, even when she was a young debutante." Grace sighed deeply. "She was just not cut out for this sort of life, I'm afraid. And she spent way too much time in the kitchen with the cook." She was misty again. "I honestly began to think she preferred her company over mine." She pressed the handkerchief to her mouth. "You know, when she was a little girl, I even told her that although I loved her, I really didn't like her." Tears sprung.

"And," she continued, "when she was a young girl, her frocks were always grass stained. Grass stained! Can you imagine? At times when I couldn't find her, I'd see her outdoors, rough housing with Cook's boys. I should have made her wear pants, but then, she probably would have loved that."

Oliver was silent for a moment, and then suggested, "Do you think that…if she's alive, she may have…well, lost her mind? Maybe," he continued, repeating himself, "she has amnesia, and she doesn't know who she is."

"Well, that would certainly be preferable to thinking she

planned all of this on purpose." Grace frowned, sending a shower of wrinkles across her face.

"Or," Oliver continued, "perhaps she's still mourning the loss of her father. That's possible, don't you think? And...and she went insane because of it."

"She was always so close to Ernest..." Grace sniffed and dabbed at her nose with a handkerchief. "Of course that could be it!"

He sat beside her once again and patted her hand. "I have hired a private detective to look into it, Grace. Leave it to me. I don't want you fretting over this."

Grace rested her head against Oliver's shoulder. "I always knew I could count on you. All those times she came to me whining because you had pushed her or scolded her and once, she even said you had hit her, I knew it was for her own good, Oliver. I never blamed you. We both knew Anastasia only too well."

After she'd gone, Oliver went to the window and looked out on his palatial lawn with its perfect gardens and clipped hedges. He had some planning to do. Lost her mind? Amnesia? Hell, no. His wife was many unpleasant things, but insanity or loss of memory was not one of them. But he could use them, for when he found her, and he would find her, he would declare her hysterical, unstable, and unable to care for herself and put her away in an asylum faster than she could call him a liar.

He poured himself another whiskey and called for his manservant to set a fire in the fireplace.

After it was done, Oliver sat back with his drink and studied the room. His room. The graduation certificate from Barleybine Prep School, a small (and nonexistent) school deep in the wilds of the Hill Country. His prestigious certificate from Oxford. The college certainly existed, but his attendance had not. His other acclaims and plaudits, all of which were well—and falsely—constructed. He had come so far. He couldn't and wouldn't let his whore of a wife mess up the life he had built for himself!

CHAPTER 12

*G*racie Jane was asleep. Tansy and Jesse sat on the settee; both held a drink. Jesse had a glass of whiskey with water and Tansy had some of Ruta's homemade dandelion wine.

Jesse spoke first. "I figure this is something monumental. That's why I thought we should have a libation first."

Tansy smiled. "Libation? Rather a formal word, don't you think?"

They both stared at the small fire in the fireplace, and finally Tansy said, "This isn't going to be easy."

"Keeping secrets never is," he answered.

She expelled a sigh. "I was so naïve. I thought I could run away from my life and simply start over again." She gave him a wan smile. "It's funny how the past keeps knocking on the door of the present."

She took a long sip of wine, felt the warmth coat her throat and then her stomach, and took another. The peaceful feeling that settled over her gave her courage.

"First let me begin by saying that by my family's standards, I am well below the ideals of normal. I mean, my mother never really believed I would find any man to marry me because I'm not—refined, among other things."

"But you did marry?" Jesse asked.

She hung her head for a moment and then met his gaze. "Yes."

"Was your husband's name John Leigh?" he asked.

"No, but please don't ask me what his name is. It's better if you don't know the details."

"And he isn't dead?"

Again she shook her head. "Although there were times when I wished he was…"

She went on to tell him things about her life. Not everything. Knowing how he felt about socialites, she kept that to herself. But she did tell him about Oliver, although she didn't call him by name. How he had been before their wedding and how he was afterwards. She spared nothing. She told him how he had charmed her, and then on their wedding night had beat her so badly she vomited just because she had spoken to a young man in the lobby of their hotel. And then he had pushed her face in the vomit before making her clean it up.

She told him of the time she yawned at a dinner with clients, and he beat her, hitting her so hard she fell against the edge of a table. The scar was still visible on her back.

She mentioned the time he caught her folding laundry. He had dragged her away, telling her they had servants for that, and then he slapped her cheek. For a week after that she wore high collars and used so much makeup she looked like a mannequin.

"He hurt me. Yes, he hurt me physically, too many times to count. I had to get away before he completely destroyed who I really am. And he deliberately tried to break down my spirit. One minute he'd call me his beauty, and the next he'd intimate that I was a cow. Can you understand why I wanted to leave?"

"I don't blame you for that," he said softly. But she noticed his hands lay fisted at his sides.

"Had you no one to speak to?"

She shook her head. "Papa died before I was married. He was my champion." She took another sip of wine. "I do resemble him in so many ways. My height, my hair, my laugh. All things my mother was forever dismayed about because I wasn't feminine."

"Did she know he beat you?"

"Oh, yes. But her answer was always, 'then stop doing what it is that gets him angry.' The only way to do that was to stop breathing—or disappear." She scrubbed her palm on the apron Ruta had loaned her. "If Papa hadn't died, I don't think Oliver would have dared treat me as he did."

"You were an only child?"

"No, I have a sister whom I love dearly." The threat of tears stung. "She didn't live nearby, but we wrote often and were close." Tears slid down her cheeks. "She's the one I miss. And to think she believes me dead, well…" She shrugged and let her tears fall onto her lap. She wiped her eyes with the back of her hand. "You can't imagine how that hurts, knowing she's mourning me, and I can't reach out to her for fear of Oliver finding out. Sometimes I miss her so much I almost can't breathe."

"Is she married?"

Tansy sniffled, wiped her nose and nodded. "He's a nice man. His name is Jacob Halloran. He's a solicitor in Atlanta."

"Was she ever aware of what was happening to you?"

Tansy shook her head. "I wanted to tell her in the worst way, and perhaps if I hadn't left, I may have tried. But I didn't want her embroiled in my misery. She has a happy life, and I wanted it to stay that way. But now…"

She sniffed again and dug into her pocket for her handkerchief. It wasn't there, so she used the hem of the apron.

"Was divorce a possibility?"

She made an unpleasant sound in her throat. "It is for a man maybe, but not for a woman. He would never have allowed it. And truthfully, I don't know what he would have done if I had tried." Besides, in her world it was not an option.

Jesse reached around and pulled her closer. She came willingly; she needed this. She needed someone to lean on, if just for a little while. And she did find him so very easy to rest against.

"It's hard to keep your head up when everyone is batting you down. I can identify with that to a certain degree."

She looked up at him, curious. "Tell me."

"When I was a kid, my cousin and I worked in the mines up

north. It was hard dirty work often dangerous." He expelled a sigh and stroked her shoulder with his palm. "One day my cousin and I were trapped by a slide. I was able to get free, but I couldn't get a good enough hold on him to pull him out. I shouted for help over and over. No one came. I had to make a decision, save myself or die with him." He scrubbed his palm over his face. "I've felt guilty ever since. When I got out and ran for help, the supervisor decided it wasn't worth risking anyone else to get him out because, after all, 'he was probably dead anyway.'"

"He died?"

"Suffocated. I still have nightmares…"

Tansy leaned her head on his shoulder. "I'm so sorry."

"And as for you," he said, winding a curl around his finger, "those people who have put you down have no idea who you really are."

She looked up at him. "They don't?"

"No."

Curious she asked, "Who am I, really?"

He chuckled. "Well, needless to say you have a mind of your own. You're spirited, strong, proud, sympathetic and a woman who is much more attractive than she thinks she is."

She pulled away and studied him. How she loved his eyes! His hair took on the lamp light, burnished like copper. His lips were parted slightly, showing the edges of his teeth. She couldn't pull her gaze away. "Once you told me I was pretty."

"No."

Her heart sank.

"You're beautiful." And then his lips were on hers, gently testing, nipping over them, then moving to her ear and back to her mouth. She opened for him, and he thrust his tongue inside, making love to her in a way she had never known. She put her hands on his chest and felt the strength there before pulling away and pressing her face against his neck.

"Oh, my," was all she could say, for her heart pounded in her chest, and her ears rang.

In bed that night she went over every bit of their conversation. And she reran the kiss in her head so many times, she wondered what would have happened if they had not stopped.

She inhaled deeply in the darkness. Jesse called her beautiful. Never in her life had anyone told her that. And how gentle he was! She had never been kissed like that before. Oliver had rarely kissed her. In fact, she didn't think he had done so since the first week of their marriage. He bypassed that part of the bedroom scene and went right to the slam bam. From what she'd heard from others, he actually treated her like a whore.

She had a sudden jolt of reality. Oliver. Even if she were to fall in love and want to marry another, she couldn't. She was already married. But she was getting ahead of herself. Marriage certainly hadn't been in her plans, nor would it be. She was a foolish ninny: One kiss from a handsome man and she was thinking about marriage!

She forced her mind to focus on something else, something that might actually help her sleep. She thought it was odd that Gracie Jane didn't have a doll. What little girl didn't have a baby doll? Well, she would have one soon enough. Tansy was happy she'd brought her old one along. On that thought, she finally fell asleep.

Jesse was coming out of the kitchen when he met Zeb in the hallway. Although he almost always stank of whiskey, he rarely seemed drunk.

"Evening, Jesse." He continued past him to the stairs.

"Zeb?" When he turned, Jesse asked, "Didn't you used to practice law in Georgia?"

Zeb scratched his scruffy chin. "Seems like a million years ago."

"Anyone you worked with still lawyering down that way?" An idea had started to percolate in his mind as soon as Tansy left him.

Zeb leaned against the newel post and crossed his arms. "No. I wasn't there very long, you know."

Jesse thanked him and went in to check on Gracie Jane, disappointed that his idea might never come to fruition.

He hadn't been shocked by Tansy's admission, but he had been disgusted and very, very angry. What kind of man gets pleasure from battering a woman? And from the little things she said, the man had money, for she mentioned servants. Had she been drawn to him because of his wealth? He'd heard of women who withstood anything just to marry up in society. By all appearances, Tansy wasn't one of them. But what did he know? She hadn't divulged everything. He knew that. What else was there?

Ellis Crawford went over his notes while he sat in the restaurant of his hotel in Topeka, Kansas. It was late; he had caught the jeweler just before he was to close his doors. When Crawford stated the purpose of his visit, the jeweler was willing to give him a few minutes.

He didn't have much to add from what Crawford already knew. The client was a woman, but without the associate's description, that was all he had to go on.

He flipped open the folder on the railroad schedule. Taking in the time it may have taken to get herself to the station, he had checked out a number of scheduled departures. Without a passenger list, he would have difficulty discovering who she was, where she was going, and when, exactly, she left Chicago.

He needed to know the number of single women traveling alone during that time. That would take some digging, but he was like an old Welsh terrier. He dug and dug and dug until he found what he wanted. He would find the woman, contact his client, and collect the remainder of his fee.

His steak arrived, blood oozing onto the plate, and he dug into the rare meat with pleasure.

 ansy made her way down the street toward the general
store. She didn't like to splurge with her funds, but she
did want a bar of that new soap the clerk had suggested when she
was in the other day. With the few extra coins she got for
tutoring Gracie Jane, she felt comfortable spending it on
something frivolous. But now wasn't that funny? She'd always had
enough money to buy whatever she wanted, and now she was
deeply concerned about purchasing a bar of soap!

The air was fine, the sky was blue, and she felt just the
slightest bite of coolness in the mountain air. She still wondered
what had become of her navy blue cashmere cape.

Speaking of which, she thought, as Margot Pine exited the
general store and came toward her. She was wearing Tansy's cape!
And appearing quite proud of it, too.

"Well, good morning, Tansy," she said as she approached.

Tansy nodded. "A good morning to you, Margot." She
studied the wrap. "That's a lovely cape."

"Oh, isn't it?" She stepped close and explained, "My Davey
found it down by the river a while back."

"And he brought it home to you? How sweet of him," Tansy
answered, having to bite her cheek.

Margot's eyes lit up. "He's such a good boy." With a little
wave, she hurried off leaving Tansy to watch as the back of her

cape swished along the boarded walk. She went in to make her purchase, then decided to drop in on the law.

Jesse looked up when she entered, a small package tucked under her arm. She had been attractive when he'd first seen her those few months ago, but since then, she'd become even more beautiful. How a woman like that wasn't aware of her beauty was a mystery to him. Her skin against her nearly black hair was white and flawless. Even the sun didn't seem able to change the color of it. And it wasn't because she was never outside. Hell, she was hardly ever inside.

"I just saw Margot Pine," she announced.

"And how is Mrs. Pine this afternoon?"

Tansy slid into the chair across from him. "Well, Mrs. Pine is quite fine, I believe, since she's wearing my navy blue cape."

Jesse groaned. "Oh, that."

She sat up straight. "You knew about it?"

He rumpled his hair and expelled a whoosh of air. "I saw her wearing it a while back and kind of thought it must be yours that you left at the river that day you arrived, but I didn't know how to handle it just then."

"Well, at first I just wanted it back, but after seeing her walk away in it, I realized she really, really loved that cape. She's probably never had something quite so…nice before."

His gaze narrowed. "Was it expensive?"

She blinked a couple of times and bit down on her bottom lip. "Oh, not so very," she said, although she wasn't convincing.

Jesse wasn't buying it. He could tell cashmere from horsehair, thanks to Judith, and Tansy's cape was definitely not horsehair. In fact, Judith had bought him a cashmere sweater early in their courtship. It was still folded up somewhere in his dilapidated wardrobe. He'd worn it once, but then realized it was too expensive to be comfortable in so never wore it again.

"So you're saying you don't want me to get it back for you?"

She had been studying the floor and looked up quickly. "Oh,

I don't think so. It's just a cape, and Margot really seems to love it."

"You might be sorry come November. It can get pretty cold up here."

She blinked again, repeatedly. "I have some funds. I will figure out something."

They sat quietly for a moment, Jesse going over the conversation he had with Zeb this morning. Zeb did not know any lawyers in Atlanta, but later he had come to Jesse and explained that he was acquainted with a priest who served in one of the Catholic parishes. He wondered if that was helpful at all. Jesse assured him it was.

"I have something I want to talk over with you. I could have gone ahead and done it without your knowledge, but under the circumstances, I think you should know."

She removed her hat and tossed it on the chair next to her. Her springy curls bounded out from beneath it, and she pushed them away from her face. "What is it?"

"Zeb is familiar with Atlanta." Immediately Tansy's eyes widened, and she paled visibly.

Jesse put his palms up in defense. "Hear me out before you faint in my office."

She straightened and brushed off her skirt. "I never faint."

He leaned forward and rested his elbows on the desk. "Would you be at all interested in getting a message to your sister?"

Again, she paled and put her hand over her mouth.

He let her process the question and waited for you to respond.

"But what if…"

"What if word gets back to your husband? It's a risk, I grant you that. But is it a risk you're willing to take?" He could almost see the wheels turning behind those bright blue eyes.

Suddenly she looked at him. "Yes. In my naiveté I thought I could live the rest of my life without any of my family, but I miss Sally so very, very much."

"We could send her a telegram."

Tansy shook her head. "No, that would be too easy to trace, don't you think?"

"All right. You take some time to think about this. When you've decided how you're going to proceed, let me know. In the meantime, I'll have Zeb get in touch with the priest who, I think, would be a good intermediary."

She smiled at him her eyes bright with tears. "Jesse Wolfe, how in the world can I ever thank you?"

He leaned back in his chair and gave her a subtle grin. "I'd kind of like a repeat of that kiss we had last night." He shoved his chair away as she hurried around the desk and dropped into his lap, putting her arms around his neck.

He knew her mouth this time and kissed her deeply, his tongue sparring with hers. Instinctively he moved his hands down her sides, his thumbs touching her breasts. She inhaled and shuddered, pressing herself closer to him. Even through her clothing he could feel hard nipples pressing against the fabric.

She broke away but rested her forehead against his shoulder; her breath came quickly. She looked up at him. Her eyes were dilated, and there was a flush from her cheeks down across the skin at her throat.

He was hard. He wanted her now and badly. "Tansy?" His voice was hoarse.

She nodded quickly. "But where—"

He stood and pulled her with him toward the open door to the back room. He took the key off the hook, shut the door behind them, and locked it. Still holding her hand, he took her to the cell farthest from the door.

They looked at each other. Jesse asked, "Are you sure about this?"

"Oh, don't ask me." She tugged at his shirt and pulled it from his jeans and then ran her fingers over his chest. "I love your chest. I love the hair." She pulled at the snaps, sending some flying across the bed. When his shirt was open, she sighed with pleasure and looked up at him, desire rampant in her gaze. "I've never seen anything so beautiful," she whispered.

He began unbuttoning her dress, fumbling with his big

fingers until she pushed them away and swiftly pulled her dress down to her waist. And then her camisole cover came off, and she tossed it across the room.

She was beautiful. Her breasts were large and firm, and the nipples stood out like little bullets. He bent and took one in his mouth, feeling her shudder. Her knees gave out, and she gripped his arms.

He grew harder, and for once he didn't attempt to tamp it down. He was hot, and he wanted her so badly he had to force himself not to throw her on the cot and ravage her.

But she took the lead. She pulled away and went to the bed. Then she reached up under her skirt and tugged off her drawers, kicking them away.

He swiftly unbuttoned his jeans, shrugged out of them, and joined her on the narrow prison cot.

"I want you naked," he whispered in her ear, blowing gently before moving away.

"Yes, yes, but not this time. I...I..." She pulled up her dress, exposing her beautiful bush of black hair, and he almost came.

He put his fingers on her mound and thrust one inside. "You are so wet." She was. He had never in his life felt a woman as ready as she was.

"For you," she whispered, spreading her legs.

He moved over her and slid into her, plunging deep, deep inside her. They lay quietly for a few moments, then he felt her shudder again, and she began to whimper and cry softly as he moved. Suddenly she expelled such a scream he had to kiss her to keep the sound from escaping into the street. Her legs locked around him, and she pushed upward, meeting his thrusts. When he realized she'd had an orgasm, he let himself discharge into her softness.

They lay together, panting, their breathing mingling. He watched her face. She looked puzzled. Perplexed. And there were tears on her cheeks. All at once she began to chuckle, quietly at first, and then louder, and the sound was so infectious he couldn't help but laugh with her.

"Aren't we something?" she asked around a winning smile.

He gave her a crooked grin. "I just couldn't have you fast enough."

"I know. Nor I you. And," she added, "I'll have you know this is the first time I ever, you know…and I really love it. I want to do it again sometime."

He chuckled and hugged her close. "It will be my pleasure, ma'am."

They were quiet, and comfortable, and neither wanted to move. Suddenly—

"Yoohoo! Sheriff, are ye in there?" Ruta's voice.

"I'm sure glad I locked the door," he whispered in her ear.

Tansy had stayed in the back until Ruta had finished with her business, which was to bring Jesse lunch. She dressed and tried to fix her wild hair. When she heard the door slam, she strolled to the front.

She peeked at the basket Ruta had brought him. "Yum. Fried chicken."

He glanced up at her, his coffee-colored eyes fathomless. "Have a piece. You must be hungry after all that exercise."

"For that, and other things," she said with a mysterious smile as she grabbed a drumstick and left him to his business.

She cleaned the meat to the bone and wished she'd taken another. But she had other plans, and a session with Gracie Jane in less than an hour.

She was just ready to toss the chicken bone in the trash by the back door when she found Ruta beside her.

"That be a chicken bone?"

Tansy gave her a faux curious look. "Does it look like one?"

Ruta chuckled. "Well, ain't you just the feisty one today?"

"Maybe a little," Tansy answered.

Ruta rubbed her chin. "Funny thing. I just dropped off Jesse's lunch. Do ye know what it was?"

Tansy feigned ignorance. "Goat cheese and buttermilk?"

Ruta gave her a glance. "Fried chicken. And if I'm any judge of my own cooking, I would bet that bone you threw in there came from the chicken I cooked this morning."

With a parting grin, Tansy said, "And it was delicious."

When she got to her room, she rummaged around for stationary, finding some in the drawer of the dresser. She paused, going to the window to look out over the river, and wondered how to begin such a letter. The willows, which she learned were called Pacific Willows, grew perhaps to waist length, no higher. So much for her thoughts of lacy weeping trees.

She searched the attic and found a small table that she had taken and now used as a desk. Her chair, for now, was a flour barrel. How unlike her polished mahogany Chippendale desk at home! Home. It was no longer her home. But what would be her home in the future? Again, she had not thought so far ahead, nor could she.

But to the letter to Sally.

My dearest Sally,

I hope you are sitting down. I am well. For you to understand my reason for falsifying my death, you must understand things that I had not yet told you. I will tell you now.

Tansy wrote and wrote, telling her sister everything, explaining why she had not told her before, and begging her not to share this new information with anyone but Jacob. Not their girls, or Mother and certainly not Oliver. Definitely not Oliver.

The only person who knew of my plight was Clarice, my maid. She saw every bruise, every break in the skin, every contusion and knew how I got them. I feel badly that she believes I'm dead, for in lieu of Papa, she was my champion.

Perhaps it sounds cruel not to inform anyone else, but time will tell. Perhaps if things change...

She finished by explaining that she could not tell her where she was, but that she was well and happy and did not regret her decision. When she finished, she had three pages filled on both sides. And she was relieved but so drained of energy she felt like taking a nap.

She found an envelope, tucked the letter inside, and put it in her pocket. It was ready to mail. It was ready for Zeb.

Now for Gracie Jane's surprise. She plucked her doll off the bed and left the room.

Jesse heard Gracie Jane's voice, pitched high with excitement, before he even entered the room. When he did, he found her with Tansy in the small parlor, and she was holding a doll.

When she saw him, she raised the doll in the air. "A doll, Papa. Miss Tansy gave me her doll!"

It was a delicate looking thing, pretty with eyes that opened and closed and a mass of dark hair, much like Gracie Jane's. But he wondered why she would have taken it with her when she left her home.

"I know that look," Tansy said. "My papa gave me that doll when I was not much older than Gracie Jane. I just couldn't bear to leave it behind."

"Maybe you knew you'd meet a little girl who needed one," Gracie Jane explained.

Tansy gave her a look of pleasant surprise. "Well, I hadn't thought of that, but it makes perfect sense."

While Gracie Jane stroked the doll's hair, Tansy took Jesse aside. She pulled the letter from her pocket and gave it to him. Leaning in, she gave him a peck on the cheek. "Thank you."

CHAPTER 14

Oliver opened the missive from Ellis Crawford, informing him of his progress. There were four women, each of whom could have been his wife. One he traced to Texas, but she turned out to be returning home from Iowa. Another left the train in Nebraska after having been in the east. The last two debarked in California, each at different small villages, one on the coast, and one inland. He was on his way to one of them as he wrote and would continue to keep Oliver updated.

Oliver's lips curled into a sneer. The bitch just couldn't get far enough away from him, could she? Oh, how tempted he was to accompany the detective on this fateful journey! But he still had business to deal with. And a few other little irons in the fire that no one else was aware of. Perhaps not altogether legal, but no one would be the wiser.

He had yet to find an outlet for his rage. He had learned to tamp it down like tobacco in a pipe. That couldn't go on forever, but he convinced himself that once he found his wife, that scheming bitch, it would all be heaped on her. He almost salivated with pleasure at the thought.

He must inform Crawford not to apprehend her. Oliver wanted the pleasure of doing that himself. He put on his hat and coat and hurried off to the telegraph office.

Sally Halloran waved as her husband carted both of their daughters off to school. She watched the runabout until it turned the corner and then closed the door. At the breakfast table, Daisy had once again asked the crucial question.

"Mama? When will Grandmamma get here? She was so sad the last time we left her. Maybe she should come live with us and not just visit." At eight, Daisy was thoughtful, introspective, and always concerned for others.

Mamie, her eleven-year-old sister, had muttered, "Grandmamma is always telling me what to do, how to dress, how to act. And she insists on calling me Mary."

"Well," her mother answered, clearing some dishes off the table, "that is what we named you."

"Then why do you call me Mamie?"

Sally wiped off the counter near the sink and put away some dishes she had drying on the counter. "My papa had nicknames for us, so I suppose that's why I have nicknames for you."

"And your name is really Sarah, isn't it, Mama?"

"Yes, Daisy, it is."

"And Grandmamma always calls me Margaret, which I don't mind at all. But Daisy is a nice name, too. I like the flower."

Mamie poked at her oatmeal, and then asked, "What was Auntie's nickname?"

Sally cleared her throat, not trusting herself to speak. After a moment, she said, "Tansy. Papa always called her Tansy. And Grandmamma will be here very soon, but she only likes to visit. She's happy where she is in spite of how we left her." Sally remembered their farewell. It was fraught with drama only her mother could provide.

"But she misses Auntie so very much," Daisy had mused.

"We all miss your Aunt Anastasia," she added. "That wouldn't change if Grandmamma lived with us." In fact, she knew it would make everyone miserable, including her mother. "And anyway, Grandmamma is very busy with her friends and her card parties and her teas. She'd have to make new friends all over again, and I don't think she would like that. She will be here in two days, so it won't be long now." Her mother's note had been almost frantic. All she had said was that she had something to share and absolutely needed to be with her.

Their maid, Kieran, poked her head out from the kitchen, breaking into Sally's reverie. "I got the laundry bundled together. It's by the back door for the pickup."

She thanked her. Just as she was about to go upstairs, there was a knock on the front door.

Kieran poked her head out again.

Sally waved her away. "I'll get it. I'm right here."

She opened the door to find a man in a clerical collar, a priest she was sure, standing on their stoop. He was pleasant looking, rather slight in stature, and had only a rim of hair circling his shiny scalp. "May I help you?"

He gave her a brief bow and then looked at her. He had kind eyes. "I'm looking for Mrs. Jacob Halloran. Sarah."

Her stomach took a little dip. "I'm Sarah Halloran. Is something wrong?"

He took an envelope from his jacket pocket. "This is for you, but before I leave it in your hands, I must ask that no one else read this except your husband. I mean no one. Do you understand?"

Puzzled and certainly alarmed, she took the missive, glanced at the handwriting, and nearly fainted. But of course she didn't. Jarvis women did not faint. She pulled herself together and invited the man in.

They sat opposite one another in the parlor, the fireplace hearth between them. Kieran popped in to ask if they needed anything, and Sally said, "No, thank you, Kieran." She thought a moment and then added, realizing she wanted the girl out of the house. "Remember that serving dish you borrowed from Mrs. Cresswell? Would you mind taking the time to deliver it to her? We've kept it too long. And while you're out, take some money from the jar in the cupboard and pick up some vegetables for supper." That would take her a little time—hopefully enough for what she was about to discover.

After the maid left, Sally, whose heart beat hard and high in her throat, opened the letter. As she read, her entire body began to tremble.

Anastasia's last paragraph was heart breaking:

If I had not left, dearest sister, he surely would have turned me into something you or I would never have recognized. Watch him, when you can. Make sure he isn't abusing Mama, or the business Papa worked so hard to leave to us. I think of you so often, miss you every day, and hope, hope that one day we can see one another.

When Sally finished reading, tears were streaking her cheeks, and she had trouble finding her voice.

"She's alive," she whispered. That was her first thought. All the thoughts that came after settled on her sister's accounts of Oliver's treatment of her. The beatings, the belittling, the quick thoughtful husband he could become after he'd struck her. The charmer he appeared to be when they were out in public. The bruises she never shared…

Sally had never really cared for Oliver. As Anastasia's older sister, she felt a great responsibility for her, knowing that their mother favored Sally and so often gave Anastasia a hard time. Oliver had always appeared aloof around them. He seemed to feel his British background was somehow superior to their American one. But he was smart and even though Sally wondered if he really cared for Anastasia, he never said or did anything to make her think otherwise.

"So, you understand why this must remain a secret." The priest brought her out of her musings.

"Yes, yes, but will I never be able to see her?"

"That is something I do not know," he answered. "But if you would like, I can deliver a letter from you to her under the guise of parish business, so the return address would not give anything away. Should someone come looking," he added with meaning. "In fact," he added, "perhaps you have some things you would like to donate to the poor? Clothing? Blankets? That could be my reason for stopping by each time."

"Yes, yes," she added quickly, already thinking of the clothing the girls had outgrown. "Can you return tomorrow? I will sit down immediately and answer her." She gave the priest a cautious smile. "We were always the best at corresponding. Rarely a few weeks went by that we didn't write one another." After a moment she said, "I miss that so very much."

She stood, and he followed her to the front door. "Until tomorrow then. Is this a good time?"

Sally nodded and watched him walk away, anxious to return to the letter and read it again. And again. Oh, Jacob would be as shocked as she was! It would be hard to keep the news from the girls, but she would force herself to do so. And Mama? That was another story. For although Mama mourned Anastasia, when and if she found out she was alive there would be hell to pay.

And how was she going to keep this a secret when her mother arrived? She must. She absolutely must. For if she was to know, she would certainly tell Oliver. He had, unfortunately, become a surrogate husband to her. Which was also very disturbing, for in her state of mind, he could very well take full advantage of her.

Ellis Crawford had a good feeling as he entered the outskirts of the little town. He liked California. Each time he came, which was quite frequent since everyone seemed to run away to the west, he wondered why he didn't stay. Maybe he would this time.

He made his way to the sheriff's office, which was tucked in the corner of a building that housed the general store. Before he got to the door, someone behind him asked, "You lookin' for the sheriff?"

He turned and found a young boy gazing up at him, a hoop, and a stick in his hands.

"Is he in?"

The boy shook his head. "He's down there fishin.'" The boy pointed to a path that led to a small river.

Anxious to question the law man, Ellis sauntered toward the river, breathing in the intoxicating smell of wild grapes.

CHAPTER 15

S ince her first foray into the river, Tansy had made time at least weekly to have a good swim. She had found a spot that was hidden from the road where the water was deep and cold. She had adjusted to the temperature. She quite enjoyed cooling off after a long, hot day.

Tansy pushed through the surface of the water to find Jesse on the shore, watching her. She grinned at him. "Do you come here often?"

"Apparently not as often as you do," he answered, his eyes never leaving her.

"Are you going to join me, or are you just gawking?" She splashed at him.

"I would, but cold water sort of…shrinks things."

Puzzled, she answered, "What things?"

He appeared embarrassed and stepped back and forth in front of her. He was actually blushing.

"Aha," she answered. "So, the bag of tricks shrinks?" She did wonder how men walked around with those things poking at their jeans.

"I'm afraid so. So you see, it probably would be just as well if you continued to entertain me from where you are."

He hunkered down and felt the water, swishing it around. "Well?"

"Well, what?" She gave him a sassy grin.

"Entertain me."

"Oh, you mean…" She pulled the top of her soggy suit over her shoulder. "…like this?"

"It's a start." He settled back on his haunches, appearing to prepare for the show.

She felt a little nervous; she'd never done a striptease before. She took a deep breath and began unbuttoning the buttons down the front of her suit.

"Come here. Let me do that."

She waded to shore, and he fumbled with the buttons, but she didn't help him. When he'd undone enough of them to pull her suit aside, he did so and revealed her breasts. Her nipples were already hard from the cold water, and they stiffened more. But instead of allowing him access, she darted away, further into the river. As she did so, her suit, heavy with water, barely hugged her hips. She wiggled around until the suit was around her ankles, then she stepped out of it, hauled it to the surface and tossed it to him.

He caught it without taking his eyes off her. "Stand up."

She stood and slowly waded toward him, her loins tingling, and her stomach flipping with dandelion fluff.

"Stop."

She did and just waited for his next command. How easy it was to do his bidding!

"Turn around."

She turned, giving him her back.

"You have a delicious rump," he murmured. "I noticed that the first day I saw you."

"My mama told me that if I didn't quit eating so much, I'd have the rump of a donkey." The sun no longer as hot as it had been in August, still warmed her. Or was it him?

"Pardon my insubordination, but your mama is wrong. Now turn back toward me."

She did, and caught his gaze, which was roaming over her entire body. "I know I'm too heavy, but—"

"Stop it," he interrupted. "Whoever put that thought in your head is a fool and an ass. You are superb. Now come here. I've got something in my jeans that requires your attention."

As she waded toward him, she boldly said, "Your bag of tricks?"

He pulled her from the water and laughed. "You've been spending too much time with Ruta." With that, he pulled her into the bushes where she saw a blanket spread out on the ground.

"You planned this? How did you know I'd be here?"

He pulled her to him. She felt his clothes rub against her bare skin, and it made her knees weak.

He whispered in her ear, nibbling as he spoke, "You don't think I've been watching you in your private little swimming hole for weeks now?"

"So you're a voyeur?" Her voice shook.

"Of a special kind. I only watch you, and now, because of all the teasing you've done, I want you so badly I think my friend down there may break the snaps on my jeans."

With newfound confidence, she pulled his shirt from his pants and unsnapped his jeans. They fell to the ground, and there, in all its glory, was his beautiful bag of tricks. A bush of very dark brown hair circled his manhood, which was tall, strong, and larger than she ever thought a man could be. It twitched at her.

"He's telling you to quit gawking and get down to business," Jesse said as he stepped out of his jeans.

They lay on the blanket, wrapped in one another's arms, while Jesse's hands roamed her back, her rear, and then her front, dipping into her wetness. Already highly aroused, she felt the stirrings inside her and gripped his penis, squeezing hard.

"That's a girl," he said with a shudder. "Now up and down slowly."

She stroked him. He was like a shaft covered in velvet. Her own wetness grew, and she said, shifting, "I think it's going to run down my legs."

He found her, and she spread for him as his fingers played with her labia. "I can't believe how wet you are."

She tried to focus on his manhood, but was having difficulty breathing, for he was stroking and dipping and gently tapping at her clitoris.

"I can feel it swelling," he whispered, continuing to stroke her.

She swallowed hard. "If you don't stop, I'll come in your hand."

He stopped briefly. "Someday I'd like you to come in my mouth."

She gasped at the thought. "Oh, Jesse, I've never…"

"Never mind," he said. "I need to get inside you before I burst."

She spread for him, drawing him into her before wrapping her legs around his back. Once he was inside, she tried to hold off, tried to keep the feeling just where it was, ready, but not quite.

Again, as before, he paused, and his breath was ragged. And then he plunged and rocked with her until she felt it, that amazing, beautiful, wonderful succulent sensation of spinning, spiraling out of control and miraculous completion. It was almost as if her heart stopped beating for just a moment.

She stared at the sky. "I never knew it could be like this."

He followed her gaze. "You mean the sky?"

She snorted a laugh and swatted him. "No, you goose. You know what I mean."

"I want you to tell me."

She turned on her side and stared into his coffee brown eyes. "I never knew people actually enjoyed this."

"This?" He ran his fingers down her stomach, into her thatch of hair.

She gasped. "Yes, this."

He dipped down and took one of her nipples into his mouth and sucked. "And this?" he said, lifting his head.

She stroked his thick, shiny hair and pressed him closer. "Yes, that too."

Afterward, as they lay together on the blanket, Tansy said, "I never realized people actually did this sort of thing outside."

He traced her stomach with a finger, gently brushing her bush. She could feel herself getting warm all over again.

"What people can do in the privacy of their bedrooms, in the dark, is much more fun when done outside, under the sun and on a blanket."

She looked at him and touched his forehead. 'You have the most beautiful eyes."

He batted them at her. "These old things? I've had them for years."

He could make her laugh so easily. "You're fun to be with, Jesse Wolfe."

He pulled her close and cupped her rump. "So are you, Tansy Leigh."

But a thought tugged at her. Was she Tansy Leigh or Anastasia Radcliffe? In her heart she wanted to be Tansy so badly it made her stomach hurt.

One afternoon when she was hanging bedding on the line, Zeb came out to help. "I appreciate this, Zeb. It's not a hard job, but it's cumbersome."

When they finished, Tansy turned to him and said, "Do you have some time?"

He laughed, a deep whiskey-rough sound that rattled in his throat. "I don't have much else these days."

She shook a rug and threw it over the clothesline. "Do you know anything about Jesse's cousin and his accident?"

Zeb scrubbed his hand over his chin. Unlike many men, Zeb's hands were finely chiseled, his fingers long and sleek. She imagined he was a good card shark. She had wondered what led him to leave his law practice.

"The mining accident?" When Tansy nodded, he said, "That was a long time ago. What do you want to know?"

Something had been gnawing at her ever since Jesse shared that story. "Do you remember the name of the mine?"

He gave her a curious look. Tansy realized that beneath his

scruffy appearance he was actually quite handsome. It was such a shame that drink took such a toll. If he were to sober up and clean up, he'd cut quite a fine figure with the ladies, for his hair was thick and tawny and had very little gray for a man his age. And he had all of his teeth. Always a plus.

"What's your interest in the mine?"

She thought a while. "My father came out here many years ago and…worked the mines," she said, fudging her facts. "Of course I don't remember which ones he worked, but I was just curious."

"Well," he began, "if I remember right, there were a couple active ones up north of here back then." He rubbed his hand over his face. "My memory isn't what it used to be, I'm afraid. But I think one of them was a Jarvis mine."

The words hit her like a punch to the stomach, and she felt a swift wave of nausea. She swallowed hard and gripped the post that held the clothesline. "Is…is that the one Jesse was working when his cousin was killed?"

"Yes, I believe it was." He gave her a puzzled look. "Does it sound familiar to you?"

He had no idea. She gave her head a little shake. "No. Thank you for the information, Zeb." She inhaled sharply. "It's time to check on Gracie Jane." As she turned to leave, she thanked him again for helping her with the bedding.

Now, not only was she a fraud, but she was the daughter of a man whose mine was responsible for killing Jesse's cousin. Things were piling up. She wasn't sure how much more she could handle before she broke down and told her entire story to Jesse.

One afternoon Zeb stopped by and handed her a letter. Her heart fluttered in her chest, her excitement was so great. She went to her room, closed the door, and sat in the old, wooden rocking chair she'd confiscated from the attic.

Sally's letter was comforting, and although she had not been aware of Oliver's behavior, she chastised her sister for not confiding in her sooner. She had wanted to know if this was forever, and if so, would they never see one another? She couldn't sugarcoat the fact that their mother's grief was real, although she didn't have to. Tansy had known it would be despite their differences.

She also appreciated their go-between, for it seemed safe for them to continue their correspondence.

When Tansy finished, she pressed the letter to her chest and rested her head against the back of the rocker. Jesse had gone to the cabin for a few days. She had longed to go with him but knew her work was here with Gracie Jane. Now, since his return, there had been an early cold spell, and snow closed the main pass over the mountains. Tansy was happy she didn't have to go outside for anything, because she certainly would have missed her cashmere cape! Fortunately, she thought with a wry twist of her mouth, Margot had come to help at the boarding house and wore it proudly every day.

And because of that purloined cape, Tansy went in search of something to keep herself warm.

Today, after seeing to Gracie Jane, Tansy went up to the attic where she had found treasures to use in her room. In a trunk tucked away under the eaves she found women's clothing.

Now, with the lamp turned high, she picked through the items. To her experienced eye, they were all expensive. She recognized many of the labels. Judith's, she guessed. And since they were probably Judith's, they were all too small for Tansy to even consider. They looked to be about the size Sally wore. But it was a shame that the material couldn't be used for something else. Clothes for Gracie Jane, perhaps? She wondered if there was a seamstress in town. She would check out that possibility.

She sat back on her haunches and thought of her own clothing. She had packed four day dresses, all of which she had worn so many times she almost couldn't stand the sight of them. She had long since discarded her corset, and her three pairs of drawers were getting pretty sad looking. Her best corset cover was torn. Tansy had never picked up a needle and thread. *My, how useless we socialites are!* What had she thought she would do when she no longer had anything to wear?

That was always taken care of by someone else, wasn't it? She had shopped, of course, that summer in Paris when they had gone abroad. But even in Paris she hadn't enjoyed it. She had wanted in the worst way to visit the Louvre. Finally, after considerable nagging, she was allowed to go with an escort.

"Tansy? Are you up there?"

Jesse's voice jolted her back to the present. Before she could put things back into the trunk, he was behind her.

"What are you doing with those things?"

She couldn't tell if he was angry or merely surprised. "Actually, I was looking for something to keep me warm." She looked up and gave him a wry grin. "Obviously these things are much too small for me."

He stood with his fists on his hips. "Judith's trunk."

"Why is it here?"

"She didn't want the items when she left. I suspect she had more than enough gowns and gewgaws back east. These items wouldn't be missed."

She couldn't read his expression, and his tone was flat. She had to ask. "Do you miss her?"

He made a growling sound in his throat. "The only good thing that came out of that relationship was Gracie Jane. There's no room in my life for someone who is so focused on herself she can't be bothered with raising a child."

"Will you tell me how it went wrong?"

He sat down beside her and pulled her into the confines of his body. She rested her head against his shoulder. To even imagine being like this the rest of her life was so impossibly wonderful she knew it could never happen.

"It was wrong from the beginning."

"What was she doing out here?" Tansy asked.

"Her pa was a higher-up in the logging business. Her ma's family had money from some business back east. I don't recall what it was. But both her folks were loaded."

Just like her, she thought. Mama had come from old Chicago

money, and Papa made his fortune in mining. At the expense, it appeared, of others. Tansy screwed up her face, grateful Jesse couldn't see her.

"The family came west to look into their logging empire. Guess they thought it would be some kind of lark, some kind of entertainment. Her ma got sick when the train stopped here, and the doc suggested she stay a while. Judith insisted on staying with her. They put up at the boarding house. Both of them had personal maids who stayed with them." He sounded truly disgusted.

"How did you meet her?"

"I was pretty new at this job, had only been the sheriff for a couple of months." He laughed softly against her hair. "Thought I was pretty damned important. When I look back on it, I must have looked like a strutting peacock. I was really full of myself."

"Were you living at the boarding house?"

He shook his head. "At that time, I was living at the jail. I had all I needed there except a place to take a bath, and Ruta always let me use the facilities. I met Judith one day as I was leaving. I took my meals there. She had twisted her ankle and needed help into the house. She was a tiny thing, no bigger than a minute."

Tansy made another face. "Why are all the desirable young women tiny?"

"Don't go there, Tansy."

She didn't argue any further. However, she and Judith were not that far apart, she was afraid. "So that's how it started? You helped her into the house?"

"Yeah, well, I actually carried her, and she made some silly comment about being carried over the threshold. At the time, I thought it was cute." He sounded disgusted with himself. "After that she put herself in my way every chance she got and pretty soon, I was feeling like the rodeo king who had roped the prize."

"So you married her."

She felt him nod. "Much to her family's disappointment. But Judith was spoiled. She always got what she wanted."

"And she wanted you."

He was quiet again and then said, "For a time. Her maid refused to stay. She up and left one day. Judith was beside herself. Couldn't do a damn thing without that girl around. Can you believe that? I guess at home where she grew up, they had maids and man servants for everything. If you were hired to do the laundry, you weren't ever asked to wait on the lady of the house." Again, he sounded both repulsed and befuddled.

"She must have felt very vulnerable when her maid left her." Knowing the way Judith was raised, Tansy actually felt a little sorry for her.

"She did nothing. She didn't lift a finger to help, not even to make our bed. By that time, we were living in one of the rooms here at the house. The only thing she ever did when she wasn't feeling sorry for herself or getting sick because she was carrying our child was play that damned piano."

Yes, we society girls certainly know how to play the piano.

"And you know the rest of it. When Gracie Jane was born, Judith high tailed it back to her rich life and left our daughter with me. Best thing she ever did for both of us."

Tansy was about to suggest they make over some of Judith's clothing for Gracie Jane, but before she got the words out, he shut the trunk and shoved it back into the corner. "I should burn that stuff for all the trouble she caused me."

They got up off the floor. The wind rattled the tiny window. "We might get some of that snow," he murmured as they left the attic.

CHAPTER 16

*T*he first thing Grace Jarvis did when she entered her daughter's foyer was sniff in disappointment and give her daughter a dramatic sigh.

"You really should have someone in to redecorate, Sarah. This wallpaper," she said, waving her gloved hand in front of her, "was here when you bought the place."

Sally took her mother's travel bag and set it by the stairs. "I liked it then, and I like it now."

Grace, wearing a mauve traveling suit with a long bodice, revealing a skirt that matched her jacket, removed her birds nest hat and placed it carefully on the bench by the front door. "You know you can afford to redecorate this entire place. Or buy a new one."

Sally was always prepared for her mother's suggestions which she rarely if ever took. "We like it the way it is, Mama. If I want to change something, believe me, I will change something." She didn't bother to mention that she preferred living on Jacob's income as a lawyer, which was comfortable, rather than throwing the fact that she had more money than he did in his face. If there ever was a dire emergency, naturally she would step up and do what was necessary.

"The girls should be in private school, Sarah."

Sally closed her eyes and took a deep breath. "They are in the finest school in Atlanta, Mama. To change them to another would only make them unhappy. They have friends and teachers they enjoy."

Sally led the way up the stairs to the guest room. "Just what is it that's so important you couldn't reveal it in a letter, Mama?"

It was quiet as Sally put her mother's things away in the wardrobe. When she turned to look at her, Grace was standing at the window. "I suppose I should wait until Jacob gets home, but I'm too upset."

She swung around, and Sally saw tears of frustration and perhaps even anger in her eyes. "Whatever is it?" Now she was concerned.

Grace shut the door and took her daughter's hand, pulling her toward the settee. "Oliver believes Anastasia is alive."

"What? How…why does he think that?" An unfamiliar cold wash of fear bathed her skin. Now Sally was terrified.

Grace took out a lace handkerchief and dabbed at her eyes. "He got a letter from a jeweler in Topeka who informed him that someone, a woman, had sold your father's watch."

Cautious, she asked, "How did they know it was Papa's?"

"There was a serial number on it." Grace continued to sniffle and wipe her nose.

"But why does he think it was Anastasia?"

Grace was clearly distressed. "Oliver was sent a list of the other items she sold. Among them was every piece of jewelry she was wearing the night she…disappeared." She picked up the decorative pillow embroidered with a huge, colorful parrot beside her and pressed it to her chest. "Somehow, she swam to safety, Sarah. If that didn't take some planning on her part, I don't know what did."

So that's how she did it. "But how is this possible?" Her voice held little conviction, but her mother didn't notice.

"I'm beginning to think I didn't know my youngest daughter at all," Grace admitted.

Cautious again, Sally asked, "So what is Oliver going to do about it?"

Grace sat up straight, her face pinched with surprise. "Is that all you have to say? What do you think of this entire scheme of hers? If she is alive, how could she do this to her family? And why?"

Composing herself, Sally took her mother's hands in hers. "Mama, if my sister is alive, she must have had a good reason to leave," she finished lamely. "At least one she thought was reasonable."

"A reason? Reasonable? What kind of reason? Oliver believes she may have lost her mind or perhaps had a bout of amnesia, or maybe suffered from melancholia after the death of your father, my dear Ernest. What other reason could she possibly have had?"

Her mother stood abruptly, tossed the pillow on the settee, and paced the room. "We had a funeral, Sarah. We had a funeral for a woman who faked her own death!" She stopped at the window again. "What will people think when they learn of this?"

Indeed, that would be her mother's biggest worry. Appearances were everything. "Oh, Mama, I wish you wouldn't work yourself up so. We don't know yet that it is Anastasia, do we? It's only speculation on Oliver's part."

Grace batted at the air, clearly frustrated. "She must have gone off the deep end, Sarah. You know she was always different. Never did as she was supposed to do as a young woman of privilege and money." She sniffed into her handkerchief. "The best thing she ever did was marry Oliver."

Sally turned away and rolled her eyes. Knowing what she now knew, Oliver was the worst thing that had ever happened to her sister.

"But why does he think she's...not herself?"

"Must I always repeat myself, Sarah? If she were in her right mind, she never would have done it. Now that I think about it, there were so many things about her that subtly pointed in that direction—"

"Oh," Sally interrupted. "That's ridiculous."

"Is it? Is it? She should have been a boy, Sarah. I've always known that in my heart she should have been a boy. She had all of your father's characteristics, and she climbed trees. Remember? She broke her arm falling from a tree! Girls don't do that. Boys do that." She took a couple quick breaths. "And…and she was always hanging about in the kitchen. Why the kitchen? Why not the music room or the salon?"

"She did use the music room, Mama. She played the piano almost daily."

Again, her mother waved the comment away. "Yes, of course, but only after she'd been out riding or hunting or doing god knows what outside with her father."

Sally was becoming more and more disturbed by her mother's behavior. If anyone was going off the deep end, she feared it was Grace Jarvis. "So what does Oliver plan to do about this hunch of his?"

"Oh, he's already hired a private detective to find her. From what he tells me, the man could be getting close."

Sally's breath caught in her throat. Could she get a missive to her sister in time? Did she dare send a telegraph? She wondered if it was possible that Oliver was having her, and her family watched. Knowing what she now knew, she wouldn't be surprised.

She forced a calm she wasn't even close to feeling and put her arm around her mother's thin shoulders. "All right let's not speak of this anymore for now. The girls will be home soon, and they don't need to hear this. Don't you agree?"

Her mother, who suddenly appeared old and tired, gave her a weary nod.

Ellis Crawford left the sheriff's office in Shale Cove disappointed. But that meant there was only one place the missing woman could be. And although he could make it there in a couple of days, he was told by the locals that they feared an early snowstorm was about to hit the mountains. If that happened, Crawford wasn't going anywhere.

He had gotten the telegram from Oliver Radcliffe which meant he didn't have to stick around once he'd found the man's wayward wife.

And, as predicted, the next morning the pass he would have taken was closed. He cursed, realizing that if he had left immediately, he might have missed it and been on his way.

Tansy looked out the window from her bed, the window at eye level. Some of the leaves were turning already. Back in Chicago she had always loved the autumn of the year. This morning the dawn was a grey blur on the horizon. All she had to do was roll over in bed, and she'd be sound asleep again.

But she knew that wasn't to be. She slid from the bed, pulled the bedding back to air it, and went to wash up. She stood there nude, ready to wash the necessary areas, when the door swung open. Before she could find something to cover herself, she saw Jesse in the doorway.

"I did knock," he said. "Ruta wanted me to ask you if you'd help her this morning."

She swung around, frantic, and reached for her robe.

"Don't," he murmured.

Two hands weren't enough to cover much, but she tried. He had seen her naked before, of course, but then she'd been aroused and prepared. "If I stand here too long, I'll freeze to death."

He strode to the bed and yanked off a blanket that was folded at the foot. He came to her slowly, appearing to memorize every inch of her, and because of his gaze and the decidedly cool room, her nipples hardened.

"You are incredible," he whispered as he got close. "You are a goddess. There are no words to describe how beautiful you are." He drew the blanket around her and pulled her close. "I want to take you back to bed. You know that, don't you?"

She put her arms around his waist, nudged her nose into his neck, and merely nodded. She felt him. He was hard against her.

"I want to touch every sweet part of your body. I want your nipples in my mouth. I want to feel the softness of your breasts against my chest. I want to find that secret spot of yours and send you into spasms of ecstasy as I watch your face. I—"

"No more, Jesse. No more, please…" She was too overcome with emotion to speak further. She thought she might cry. A part of her wanted desperately to allow him to continue. A need for him consumed her, and she fought for self-control.

As he held her, she wondered, very briefly, what would happen if he ever learned the truth about her?

It was like a dream…only it was real. As much as she knew she had fallen in love with him, she was beginning to realize that a future, without a miracle, was not possible.

After he left her, she dressed in one of her more work worn dresses. She had promised to help with the laundry again.

She got downstairs to find Margot waiting for her, her expression rather down. "What is it?"

Margot had scrub brushes and a pale of soapy water ready to use on the parlor floor. "It's Bert. He just can't shake that cough. He's had it for months now."

"Oh, Margot, I'm sorry. Has the doctor been there?"

She nodded. "He's done all he can. Time will tell, I guess."

"Would you rather go home? I can do this."

"No. The doc says it's best not to be around Bert too much. I sent Davey over to the Parnells for a couple of days, and I'll be here working, so Doc said he'd check in on him.

CHAPTER 17

*G*race had stayed at her daughter's a week. Although she was able to keep silent about her news when the girls were around, she continued to harp on it when she and Sally, and sometimes Jacob, were alone.

One afternoon when her mother was resting, Sally wrote a quick note to her sister. It read: *Oliver knows you're alive! A detective is on the way. Flee!* She had sent the maid to the rectory under the guise of delivering blankets. The letter was tucked into Keiran's apron pocket.

Sally was certain that by the time her mother had left, she had completely convinced herself that Anastasia had gone crazy. And that, with Oliver's similar concern, could definitely put her sister in a place she didn't want to be if found.

Although she knew Kieran would do it, Sally stripped the bedding and folded the blankets, returning them to the armoire. The girls had done their homework and were in the room they shared. Sally heard them chatting. They hadn't gone to sleep yet and the clock in the foyer had chimed eight.

She left the guest room and poked her head into their room. "It's time to douse the lamp, girls." She went to each one and kissed them on the forehead, something she had done since the day she brought each of them home.

"I'm glad Grandmamma was here, but I'm also happy she

went home. I think she was glad to leave as well, don't you, Mama?" Daisy, always thoughtful.

"She has two parties and a tea to prepare for. She was happy to leave." She blew them a kiss and left them, closing the door behind her.

Downstairs, Jacob was waiting in the parlor. He handed her a sherry, which she gratefully accepted. She settled on the sofa beside him and rested her head against his shoulder.

"Your mother is going to have a stroke if she keeps going on as she is."

Sally took a sip of wine, allowing it to warm her tongue and mouth before swallowing it. "I certainly don't blame Anastasia for what she's done, but if she knew how disturbing Mama's thoughts are, she might think twice about staying away."

"I've checked into the law regarding institutionalization," Jacob began, "and at least now days there's a trial, whether it does any good or not, I couldn't say. I would suspect the outcome isn't good for the person on trial, especially if it's a wife."

She turned toward him. "What if he finds her? And he will find her unless she receives my urgent letter and has time to run again."

"Is that the kind of life you want for your sister? Always on the run?"

"Certainly not, but Jacob, she couldn't have thought this through very clearly. Surely she must have wondered what would happen if Oliver caught her. Of course, he would have every right to drag her back here and do whatever he wishes with her. He's already planted the seed that she's crazy."

"And your mother is vulnerable, especially now. She could easily be convinced to testify against Anastasia's sanity, especially if she's already been prodded to believe your sister went crazy because her father died."

They sat quietly, sipping their drinks, each having thoughts that both worried and frightened them.

Oliver tapped the letter against his chin. His emissary in Atlanta didn't have much to say unfortunately.

Grace had been home a week and now sat across from him in the wing chair by the fireplace, doing needlepoint. She always seemed to need to have her hands busy. "Is there any news?"

"I've had a man in Atlanta watching Sarah's house—"

"Why?" Grace interrupted. She put her hand work in her lap and gave him a harsh look.

"I thought Anastasia might get in touch with her."

"How would you know? I was there a week and didn't see anything out of the ordinary."

"Covering bases, that's all. At any rate, he says there isn't much activity there, the maid running errands, a priest picking up clothing, I assume for the poor." He walked to the window and focused on the treetops, which were swaying in the wind. "All the normal activities, the girls going to school, Jacob at work." He swung around. "Are they Catholic?"

"Jacob is. We, of course, are Presbyterian as you know."

He did know, and now, as part of the family, he was forced to attend the dry as dust church service every Sunday. He had yet to find a way to get out of it, but he would keep trying. If nothing else, it made him look good. At the funeral he had received so many whispers of sympathy he nearly told all of them to stick a bloody sock in it. Often, his thoughts came out in the cockney language of his youth. That should have reminded him where he came from, but it only made him more conscious of his need to cover it.

"Why wouldn't she collect things for her own parish?" he wondered.

"Oh, I don't think we do much of that on a regular basis. She said she'd been giving things to Jacob's priest for quite some time. He came by one day while I was there. Nice enough fellow; not pompous, just very pious."

Oliver knew he was grasping at straws, trying to find anything that might give him an edge on finding his treacherous wife. In the meantime, he was getting behind not only in the job at the mining office, but his other, personal projects as well. And that wouldn't do.

"I find it hard to believe Anastasia hasn't attempted to get in touch with her sister."

Grace glanced up, giving him a half smile. "Maybe she isn't as crazy as you think she is."

Oliver wasn't sure she was crazy at all, but he was going to make damned sure the courts thought she was when he got his hands on her.

CHAPTER 18

Journal Entry: I have noticed that the crow is more adaptable to human surroundings while the raven is less social, more cautious.

Crows instigate nearly 97% of altercations between crows and ravens, particularly during breeding. Crows will often come together and gang up on a pesky raven to keep it from their nests.

*J*esse had been out making rounds of the nearby ranches. When he returned and opened the door to the jail, he found Lloyd behind the desk, his eyes so big he was afraid they might pop out of his head. He was just about to ask him what was wrong, when…

"Hello, Jesse."

His heart rate soared, and his stomach pitched to his knees. "What the hell…"

"A pleasure to see you as well," Judith replied.

He turned and found his ex-wife sitting primly on one of the office chairs, her hands folded on top of her skirt and her back ramrod straight. Her light hair was styled perfectly, and the hat was a wasteful collection of feathers. She wore a dark green traveling suit. An umbrella rested against the chair. She was still a pretty little thing, but that fact didn't move him at all.

"What are you doing here?"

She appeared surprised. "Why, I'm here to see our daughter."

His gaze narrowed, and he was hard pressed not to punch his fist through something. If not her, then the wall.

"Why now?"

She dipped her chin and gave him what passed for a sympathetic smile. "Perhaps I should have given you some warning, but I was afraid I might not find her here if I had."

Lloyd threw them both a wary look and crept out, leaving Jesse to close the door behind him. "What is it you really want?"

She gave him an exaggerated sigh. "Well, truth be told, I have many things I want for our daughter. First and foremost, however, is this…there is a new invention making all the medical news. It has even reached San Francisco. It's a machine called an x-ray, and it takes pictures of people's bones right through the skin and everything."

"I heard about it," he answered, for Doc Grossman had mentioned it to him one day when he'd checked on Gracie Jane.

Her perfectly arched eyebrows went up. "Really? Here in the sticks?"

If she was itching for a fight, he wasn't going to give it to her. "So what about it?"

She squirmed on the uncomfortable seat. "I have an appointment to take our daughter there next week to see what's wrong with her legs."

There was a roaring in his ears, and he could barely hear himself when he shouted, "You what!"

"You heard me, Jesse. If there's a chance she can be helped, don't you think it's worth taking?"

God. She was sounding logical. This didn't bode well. His heart still hammered in his chest, his breathing was erratic and shallow, and he was sweating. Was this what it felt like to have a heart attack?

"So, let me get this straight. If they could find out what is wrong with Gracie Jane's legs and could fix them, you would do what exactly?" He could feel his rage growing.

She *tsked*. "Gracie Jane. How I dislike the sound of that. It makes her sound so common."

"She's six. She's gone by that name since she was a baby. Anyway, you're changing the subject."

Judith stood and walked demurely to the window and studied the street. "This is a one horse town, Jesse. It always has been. I think it's time for our daughter, Grace, to live the life she was born to live. With me...in Boston."

"The hell you say!" Blood rushed to his face, and his words rattled the windows.

She turned and looked at him. "I can give her all the things you can't, Jesse."

"She's got everything she needs right here." He was, however, a tiny bit afraid. Had he known this day might come? Hell, yes. Had he prepared for it? Hell, no. Because it wasn't going to happen. He calmed himself.

"So what if this newfangled machine shows that nothing can be done? Then what? You shuttle her back here with me? That is," he added, "if I let you take her away in the first place."

She had the decency to look away. "I admit I've been a very bad mother. But I've changed, Jesse. I was always too busy worrying about myself. Then I realized that I actually had this beautiful daughter, and suddenly I wanted her with me, to watch her grow even if she can't be active like other children."

"Then move here," he suggested.

She actually snorted a laugh, then covered her mouth with her gloved hand. "You aren't serious. Boston is where a young debutante belongs, Jesse. And the doctors are specialists, not like your doctor here, who probably treats horses and pigs as well as people."

"No, no, no, no!" He pounded on the desk so hard the papers that were stacked on it fluttered to the floor. "I don't believe you. You don't even know what it is to care for her."

"I have plenty of people to care for her. I have a staff of over twenty," she told him.

"And when things get hard, you'll foist her off on one of

them. When you get bored with your new toy, you'll impose on your help once again."

"Well, of course, I'll have help. My god, Jesse, even you have help. I assume your aunts are still about, caring for the girl. And there's always that Ruta person, who, if you'll pardon me saying so, isn't such a good example for a young girl."

Suddenly the door flew open, and Tansy rushed in. "Jesse, I—"

She looked from Jesse to the petite woman standing near him and stopped. "Am I interrupting something?"

Judith narrowed her gaze and looked Tansy up and down. "And who might you be?"

Tansy squared her shoulders and stepped up to Judith, took the tiny hand in hers and gave it a good shake. "Tansy Leigh. I'm Gracie Jane's tutor."

Judith pulled her hand away, whirled and stared at Jesse. "She has a tutor?"

Gathering himself, and grateful for Tansy's timely interruption, he answered, "You didn't expect me to live out here and not have my daughter educated, did you?"

Judith crossed her arms over her small chest. "That doesn't change things, Jesse. I have an appointment with the doctor in San Francisco next week, and I intend to take Grace with me."

Tansy appeared to brighten. "You mean an appointment for her legs? Oh, Jesse. That's a wonderful idea. Why don't I accompany them? Gracie Jane should have someone with her who is familiar with her daily routine, don't you think?" She turned and gave Judith an innocent, wide-eyed smile. Jesse had to bite his lip to keep from smiling.

"I have help," Judith said, dismissing her.

"If you insist on doing this, Judith, I must insist that Tansy go along to be with Gracie Jane. It's bad enough that you want to tear her away from all she's known, the least you can do is let Tansy be there to give her moral support."

Judith was quiet, obviously weighing her options. "I suppose I have no other choice."

Tansy, smiling brightly, asked, "When do we leave?"

"The next train for San Francisco leaves the day after tomorrow. I expect you to have Grace ready and at the station by eight." With that, she picked up her umbrella and gracefully moved toward the door and stopped, as if waiting for someone to open it for her.

"Where are you staying?" God, he hoped not at the boarding house.

She gave him a superior smile. "I have a private car on the train. We will be traveling to San Francisco in it. It's quite comfortable." Again, she waited at the door.

Tansy said, her voice over eager, "Oh, here. Let me." She opened the door wide as Judith gave Jesse a glance that shot daggers.

After she'd gone, Tansy and Jesse looked at each other. Tansy's innocent, wide-eyed bearing was gone, and she narrowed her gaze at the door. "I met Lloyd as I was crossing the street, and he looked as if he'd seen a ghost. So that's Judith."

Jesse smacked his first against his palm and paced. "I don't want this, but how can I say no? I knew that her money would someday come back to bite me in the ass."

Tansy rubbed her hand down his arm. "What else does she want?"

After a long moment, Jesse answered, "She wants to take Gracie Jane back to Boston with her." He was terrified and wasn't afraid to show it. "I can't let that happen. Her family has money and power, and I've got..." He threw his arms up, indicating the jail. "This is what I've got."

She leaned into him. "Let's do this one step at a time. We'd better both go and tell Gracie Jane what's happening. Hopefully, knowing that I'll be with her, she won't worry as much. But I will say," she added, "it's not a nice person who is willing to take a child away from the only parent she has ever known. Of course, I don't know Judith personally at all, but that is a very selfish trait."

Jesse pulled Tansy into an embrace. "You have no idea."

Ruta took sick for a couple of days, and Margot Pine took her place in the kitchen. She was a very fine cook. While Ruta's fare was always basic with meat and potatoes smothered in a lot of gravy, Margot took time to put together some wonderful squirrel and venison stews swimming in, instead of gravy, savory sauces and lots of garden vegetables. Her bread wasn't as good as Ruta's, but no one complained.

Tansy couldn't believe she had actually eaten squirrel! If her mother knew, she would, indeed, faint for the first time in her life.

To no one's surprise, Judith was not welcomed with open arms when she made her visit to the boarding house. Tansy watched as she preened around the parlor, raising her nose in the air at the sparse furnishings. She even had the audacity to wipe her gloved hand over the top of the piano and found dust on it when she pulled her hand away. She shook her head, brushing her hands together to dislodge it.

Tansy and Ruta, who still didn't feel well but wouldn't miss a confrontation with Gracie Jane's mother, watched her from the kitchen. Tansy had filled her in on the reason for Judith's visit.

"Same snooty bitch," Ruta said under her breath. "She's got some nerve sashaying back into our lives, threatening to take Gracie Jane away."

Tansy was worried. If, as Judith planned, she took Gracie Jane all the way back to Boston, what could Jesse do about it? She didn't know the law, but perhaps Zeb did. She left the kitchen and found him outside on the back porch, smoking his pipe. The smell was sweet and spicy. It reminded her of her father.

"Zeb? I have a question."

He merely nodded and studied her.

"Do you know what the law is concerning the rights of a father in obtaining permanent custody of a child?"

He nodded slowly. "Had a case myself many years back."

Eager to hear, she said, "Tell me about it."

"Not much to tell. Fathers don't get much sympathy in the courts, I'm afraid."

That wasn't good news. "Is there some law?"

He took out his pipe and put it in the ashtray on the small table next to him. "Common law in the United States is in favor of the mother's custody. That's the law from the Philadelphia Court of General Sessions."

Disappointment washed over her. "Is there no case where the father can gain custody?"

He nodded and said, "On the basis of drunkenness, and it can be proven, or if she's mentally or physically unfit. That's about it."

"In the case of all children?"

He shifted in his chair and returned the pipe to the place between his teeth. "Mothers always get custody of daughters, or weak or disabled children, and, of course, young children."

She sank into the chair beside him. "Then I don't see any way Jesse is going to be able to keep Gracie Jane with him."

Zeb eyed her with sympathy. "It doesn't appear likely."

"But what about the rights of the child? What if Gracie Jane doesn't want to go with her? Has she no say in the matter?"

Zeb shook his head. "You know," he began, "living in Boston has a lot of advantages. She would be surrounded by everything a young girl needs to become an accomplished woman."

Tansy snorted a laugh. "All the advantages in the world don't mean happiness."

"And you know this from experience, I presume?" He cocked an eyebrow and gave her a questioning look.

She merely answered, "Happiness outweighs everything." Or did it?

The doctor had been in to check on Ruta's recovery. "There's been influenza spreading through the country. I've had updates weekly about cases everywhere from Boston to San Francisco." He glanced back at the door. "She doesn't have it, but I fear others in town may come down with it."

Jesse spoke up. "Tansy and Gracie Jane are going up to San Francisco with my ex-wife, Judith, to see about that new x-ray contraption. When she returns, I'll take Gracie Jane to the cabin until things settle down around here." He wanted to believe it. He didn't know what he would do if Judith forced his hand.

He saw the doctor out and glanced at the snow-spattered peaks of the mountain range. He hoped it wasn't going to be an early winter.

When they arrived at Judith's private train car, Tansy was impressed. At least the woman understood that the child needed comfort for such a long trip. Or perhaps it was for her own comfort.

After Tansy had settled an anxious Gracie Jane in for a rest, she joined Judith in the main part of the car. Judith looked at her sharply. Tansy asked, "Is there something wrong?"

"You are no more a tutor than I am a scullery maid."

Tansy fussed with her hair, trying to tame it. "Why do you say that?"

"Oh, you may come across as a modest, unassuming woman, but I know a debutante when I see one because, as you know, I am one. And," she continued, "the doll you gave my daughter is very expensive. I mean, *very* expensive. It has a porcelain face, not wax. If it wasn't yours, how did you come to have it?"

Tansy stared out the window at the passing landscape. Indeed, it was far more pleasant in this car than it had been when she'd taken the train with the 'rabble' as some called them. "What does it matter what I am?"

Judith picked up her needlepoint and began to work a colorful bird pattern on the fabric. "It doesn't matter to me. I am curious, however, as to your relationship with Jesse."

"Why should that bother you?"

Judith smoothed her hand over her skirt and shrugged. "It doesn't bother me personally, but I know Jesse. Because of me, he absolutely despises women with status and money."

Tansy inhaled, exhaling slowly, recalling everything Ruta had told her. "I know."

"So he doesn't know who you really are." It wasn't a question. "I guess my question would be, what on earth are you doing in that one-horse town, passing yourself off as a tutor?"

Tansy continued to stare out the window and then tossed her a glance. "It's a long story."

Judith looked up from her handwork and gave Tansy a poignant look. "It's a long ride."

And so, by the time they reached the station in San Francisco, Tansy had related most of her story to her lover's ex-wife, which she thought was extremely odd, indeed. There were things she kept to herself, such as who she really was. Judith didn't need that for ammunition if, indeed, she chose to use it.

Judith gave her a cynical smile. "If you have any interest in sharing a life with Jesse, I don't see how this is ever going to work."

"I know that, too."

Later, as she tried to rest, she began to feel a little queasy. Maybe she was getting a touch of whatever ailed Ruta.

Judith had gotten a suite for them at the Palace Hotel, the tallest building in San Francisco, with its white columned balconies and spectacular lobby. To Gracie Jane's delight, there was an elevator, or a rising room, red wood paneled, which was moved by hydraulics. To the child, it was like magic.

The suite itself was plush and luxurious with a large bay window looking out over the city. Their appointment was for the next morning, and everyone, especially Gracie Jane, was a bit uneasy.

Judith, who, Tansy discovered, was actually quite good with her daughter, had sat down beside her and told her about the visit. "The doctors don't know if it will show us anything helpful, so I don't want you to get too hopeful."

Gracie Jane's brown eyes were big and bright. "I can't help it. I just can't help it."

Tansy watched the conversation unfold.

"You enjoy living with your papa, don't you?" There seemed to be some pain in her voice, or perhaps Tansy imagined it.

Gracie Jane looked at Judith. "Where else would I live?"

Tansy's stomach cramped as she waited for Judith's answer.

Judith took one of Gracie Jane's curls and looped it around her finger. "I was kind of hoping you would come back to Boston and live with me."

Gracie Jane's face fell, and her eyes filled with tears. "But... what about Papa? Could he come, too?"

"Sweetheart, I don't think we could get your father out of that one horse town with a stick of dynamite strapped to his back."

The girl glanced at Tansy who tried to keep her expression bland. "But...but I couldn't live some place if Papa wasn't there."

"You know," Judith continued, "back where I live, we have horses. Wouldn't you like to have your own pony?"

Tansy turned away and rolled her eyes. Why did every parent think their child wanted a pony? Oh, she loved horses, but she also knew how much work it took to care for them properly.

Gracie Jane shook her head. "I can't ride a horse. My legs are too weak. And...and today my ankles hurt."

Tansy had noticed that when she put Gracie down for a rest. Her ankles were swollen. Last week it had been her knees.

Judith smiled down at her. "Maybe tomorrow we'll discover there's a way to make them strong again."

Gracie Jane's tears welled up again. "But I won't go with you if Papa doesn't come."

Tansy realized that Judith probably knew that the law was on her side, but she wisely didn't share it with her daughter.

Judith patted her daughter's arm. "Let's not fret about it now. Are you hungry? Let's order some dinner, shall we?"

Later in the evening as Tansy prepared for bed, she heard Gracie Jane sobbing quietly into her pillow. She sat down beside her. Gracie Jane looked up at her, eyes red, nose running. "I don't want to go away."

Tansy lay down next to Gracie Jane and curled her body around hers. "And we don't want you to go either, sweetheart."

"She can't make me, can she?"

Tansy inhaled deeply. What to tell her? Certainly not the truth.

As it turned out, the x-ray machine showed that Gracie Jane's joints were, indeed, inflamed. The doctor, a specialist himself, told them that along with her patch of crusty skin, which he called psoriasis, Gracie Jane's diagnosis was Juvenile Rheumatoid Arthritis.

When he asked what sort of treatment, if any, she received, Tansy told him of the oat paste, and he nodded his approval. He also added that aloe vera, a succulent plant with medicinal purposes, would be helpful topically as well.

He insisted they continue putting her through exercises to keep her legs limber. Too often, he told them, children end up crippled for life because they hadn't been given the proper care.

The trip back to Willow River was a quiet one, the biggest excitement was that Gracie Jane had lost a tooth. But Tansy wondered what the crafty Judith might have up her sleeve now.

hen they arrived, they learned that Bert Pine had died of pneumonia. Margot and Davey were having a hard time with it, as was to be expected. Margot would stay on at the boarding house to help Ruta with all the work. Davey stayed with the Parnells.

Jesse found the travelers in the parlor having tea and fresh cookies.

"Papa!" Gracie Jane sat with her arms stretched out, waiting for a hug. Jesse strode to her and gave her a hug.

"I've missed you, sweetheart," he murmured.

"Me too, Papa, me too. But look," she said, pointing to her mouth. "I've lost a tooth!"

He peeked into her mouth, and sure enough, on the bottom, was a hole where a tooth used to be. "Well, I'll be."

"I felt it moving even before we left home, but it wasn't until I got on the train again that it really moved a lot." She dug into the pocket of her frock. "Here it is." She offered it to her father with a flourish.

He took it from her and slid it into the pocket of his shirt. "I'll have to do something very special with this, won't I?"

"And I'm gonna lose a whole bunch more!"

"So you'll be toothless, just like Walt. Is that it?"

She laughed at such an idea.

Judith cleared her throat. "I see the piano is still here. Do you play?" she asked Tansy.

"I do indeed, but Gracie Jane has also learned to play. Haven't you, dear?"

Gracie Jane grinned. "I can play some songs."

Judith, who actually appeared interested, asked her to play one for her.

When Gracie Jane had finished, Judith said, "*Ode to Joy* by Beethoven. Very impressive, Grace."

Margot appeared at the door. "Gracie Jane? Shall we get you ready for bed?" The girl waved happily to everyone as she left, oblivious to the dialogue that was to begin when she was no longer in the room.

"Well," he began. "Let's hear it."

Tansy looked at Judith who took the lead. "Grace has a child's form of arthritis. Her knees, ankles and hips are affected, although not at the same time. Sometimes, I'm told," she said, looking at Tansy, "she has no pain at all. When that happens, she can walk as well as you or I."

He frowned. "I didn't know…"

"Well, now you do. Jesse, there are so many wonderful doctors in Boston who can treat this type of thing. I really wish—"

"Don't wish for something that isn't going to happen, Judith." His words sounded brave, but he didn't feel brave at all.

Tansy dared to speak. "Now that we know for certain what it is, we know how to treat it," she said. "She doesn't need to go to Boston for that."

Judith gave them both a stubborn look. "You do know it's my right to take her with me."

"You have no rights!"

Tansy put a hand on his arm. "She does, Jesse. It's the law. It doesn't matter that she has abandoned Gracie Jane for six years. It doesn't matter that as a mother, she is utterly disgraceful. It doesn't matter that she has had no interest in Gracie Jane until this very moment. All that matters is that the law will always side with the mother in cases like this."

Despite the jabs against her person, Judith puffed up. "She's right, you know."

Jesse cursed and paced the room. What could he do? He couldn't lose his daughter. Not to Judith. Not like this.

"It might help you to know," Tansy said, interrupting his thoughts, "that Gracie Jane doesn't want to live anywhere unless you're there with her."

Judith shot her a nasty look.

The silence in the room was so great Jesse could hear his heart beat.

Tansy stood. "This is between the two of you. I'll check on Gracie Jane and then go upstairs."

They both watched her leave. Judith broke the silence. "She's quite a woman, your tutor."

He swung around and looked at her. "What's that supposed to mean?"

Judith poured herself another cup of tea, stirred in a lump of sugar, and took a sip. "She's a mystery to you, isn't she?"

"She doesn't have to tell me anything," he murmured.

"Oh, don't tell me you haven't wondered about her, Jesse. Does she really seem like a tutor to you?"

"I don't know. I've never met one before," he said, his voice edged with sarcasm.

"Well I have, and trust me, she is not a tutor."

He grabbed a pillow from the sofa and tossed it across the room. "What do you know about it?"

Judith daintily put her cup on the saucer. "You'd be surprised how forthcoming she was when it was just the two of us alone."

"So who is she?" God, why didn't he just tell her to mind her own business?

Judith dabbed at her lips with a napkin. "I don't know *who* she is, but I know *what* she is."

"And how is it that you have so much insight into someone you just met?"

"Suffice it to say, dear Jesse, that she grew up in circumstances quite similar to mine."

"If you're trying to piss me off, you're doing a damned fine job." She was just trying to get under his skin. She'd always been good at that. "And believe me, the two of you are nothing alike."

She laughed, that tittering little sound he remembered well. "For that I'm eternally grateful. I knew a couple of debs when I was younger who were tall like she is, and they had great difficulty finding a suitor. Trust me."

"You've lived in a very superficial world, haven't you?" He was on the defensive, and he didn't like it. "What else did she tell you?"

Judith stood and straightened her skirt. "Oh, no. If you want to know more, you'll have to ask her yourself. Now, I think I'll retire as well. We can discuss Grace's future in the morning."

After she left, he put out the lamp and sat in the dark. There was something different about Tansy lately. When she wasn't aware he was studying her, she had such sadness in her eyes he couldn't bear it. Was Judith right? Was Tansy hiding her wealth from him? Early on in their relationship he harped on Judith's money, her selfishness, her neglect of Gracie Jane. That alone would have made Tansy reluctant to share her whole story.

They had met one night after everyone was asleep, took a blanket, and went out to look at the stars. He couldn't keep his hands off her, and she appeared to need him as well. Yet after they had made love, she got quiet, unlike the other times.

He'd asked her what was wrong.

She had nuzzled close to him, assuring him everything was fine, that she was merely tired. He had wanted to believe it. Although her words didn't ring true, there was something else.

Maybe she was tiring of him. He was familiar with that feeling, for with Judith it had happened quickly. Once they were married, she didn't want to sleep with him anymore, claiming that all married couples had separate bedrooms. Hell, what did he know? He didn't want to believe that of Tansy. The more he was with her the more he wanted her. He thought she had felt the same. What if, in spite of everything, she was just another woman, having a fling with a bumpkin of a sheriff?

The thought had hit him hard, and he couldn't quite convince himself that he was wrong.

The next morning Judith summoned Jesse to her train car. He went with a great deal of trepidation. He found her sitting at a small table, a tray of baked goods and a pot of coffee in front of her. She motioned him to sit. "Help yourself to breakfast."

He ignored her, although the coffee smelled good, unlike Ruta's. But his stomach was in knots, and nothing would untie them.

"I've come to a decision," she announced.

He was at her mercy. He despised the feeling of helplessness she lorded over him.

"Let me say something first," he said. "Yeah, the law is on your side. But in my mind, you only want to take Gracie Jane away from me because you're selfish and always have been. What is she to you? Some kind of trophy? She's a sweet little girl who is in pain much of the time. She doesn't deserve it. She also doesn't deserve to be uprooted from all she's ever known and taken to a place completely foreign to her. If you do this, you will break her heart. And mine."

"And what about me, Jesse? Am I supposed to fall to my knees and beg your forgiveness for wanting to raise our daughter in comfort? I can do so much more for her—"

"Hold it right there," he interrupted, simmering. "Now that we know what she suffers from, we can treat her here. And, if need be, we can take her to San Francisco to see the specialist from time to time to make sure she's doing all right." He was quiet for a moment and then added, "It's not in my nature to beg, Judith, but I am begging you. Don't take her away from me."

Judith raised an eyebrow as she studied him. "If you had continued to rant and rave, I would have been hard pressed to accommodate you. However," she added, pouring herself some coffee, "since you beg so nicely, I'll let her stay with you."

The relief he felt was overwhelming. "Thank you. And before you change your mind, I'll leave. If you want to say goodbye to Gracie Jane, she's probably in our small parlor with her tutor." He dug his pocket watch from his shirt pocket and glanced at it. "This is the time she usually reads to her."

Judith snickered. "Oh, yes. Her 'tutor'."

Ellis Crawford finally made it over the pass into the small valley town of Willow River. He was eager to find the sheriff. If this turned out to be what he hoped, he had finally bagged the badger, so to speak.

He found the sheriff's office and went inside. Sitting behind a battered desk was a fellow who looked like someone had taken an egg beater to his hair. Dark tufts stuck out all over. "You the sheriff?"

The kid, for he was just a kid, jumped up from behind the desk, hitting his head on the lantern that hung above it, sending it swinging from side to side. "No, sir. I'm his deputy, Lloyd Johnson." He stuck out a meaty hand, and Ellis took it. The kid had a firm grip anyway.

"Is the sheriff around?"

The deputy shook his head. "He'll be back tomorrow, I expect." The lad studied him. "Something I can do for you?"

Ellis considered it. But did he really want to explain everything twice? "I think I'll wait on the sheriff, if you don't mind. Meanwhile, is there any place that can put me up for the night?"

The deputy scratched his head, making the hair stand out in all directions even more. "There's a boarding house down the street. A big white house. You can't miss it. Sometimes they have rooms available. Take a left out the door, and it's just beyond the general store."

Ellis thanked him and left. Traveling that damned pass had tired him out. He was looking forward to a clean bed and some grub.

Margot Pine was in the process of taking the potato peels to the compost pile when the doorbell rang. She appeared to be the only one around. She dumped the peelings into a bowl and went to the door, wiping her hands on her apron in the process. She opened the door, and there stood a tall fellow with hair the color of her departed mister. She teared up, sniffled and wiped her face with the back of her hand.

"Is something wrong, ma'am?"

Oh, and he had a voice like Bert's too...that little bit of leftover Irish! She waved away the question. "I'm so sorry. It's just that...my mister died recently, and you...you remind me of him."

He apologized, sounding very sincere, and then said, "I hate to interfere with your grieving, but I'm looking for a room for a few nights."

Margot pulled herself together and opened the door wide, inviting him in. "I do apologize. I don't usually go to pieces in front of strangers." She thought a moment about his request, and since she appeared to be the only one in charge at the moment, added, "We do have a room. Would you like to see it?"

"That won't be necessary, ma'am. Just point the way. And if you would be so kind as to let me know when supper is served, I'd be much obliged."

As she left him, Miss Tansy opened her door. "Margot? I'm feeling a bit squeamish today. I think I'll skip supper."

"Well, I'll bring you some broth and flatbread, dear, in case you feel like eating later."

"And, Margot? I hate to ask, but can you check in on Ruta? I know she's better, but she still needs help with some things."

Promising to do so, Margot returned to the kitchen to prepare for the evening meal, still thinking about the new boarder.

Tansy was indeed feeling a little squeamish, just as she had on the train ride to San Francisco. It was probably just a touch of something. She had no symptoms that caused her any great concern. But she had regretted telling Judith so much about her past. No doubt she shared it with Jesse, who already knew that much anyway.

She flopped onto the bed and put her arm over her eyes. She loved a man who had no idea who she really was. He had no idea that his cousin died in one of her father's mines, basically ignoring Jesse's pleas for help. Even if Judith had told him Tansy came from privilege, he would have no idea that she grew up not wanting for a single thing. Trips abroad were as normal as trips to the beach. She was an heiress to a mining fortune, not to mention the money her mother would leave her and Sally once she was gone. She was, in fact, everything he hated in a woman. He as much as told her that when he spoke of Judith. And, perhaps most of all, she, herself, was still a married woman.

She knew he cared for her, perhaps not love, but certainly something close to it. How would she possibly handle any kind of explanation? He would be hurt, probably even disgusted. Definitely angry, as if she had set out to dupe him on purpose. And she would leave him. She would have to.

CHAPTER 20

*W*hen Jesse arrived at the jail the following morning, he found a man waiting for him. The man stood and offered his hand. He was tall, almost as tall as Jesse. His hair was a sandy brown, perhaps forty, in good shape, and well dressed. Jesse shook his hand.

"Ellis Crawford, Sheriff. I was hoping to have a word with you."

Jesse nodded and went around to his desk, avoiding the lantern as he sat down. "So what is it I can do for you, Mr. Crawford?"

The man picked up a briefcase that was on the floor beside him and rifled through it. "I've been hired by a man in Chicago to find his wife."

An alarm went off in Jesse's brain. "And what makes you think she's here?"

"I've tracked a woman this far. Actually, I followed up on a few, but this is the last one. If I don't find her here, I can't imagine where she would be."

"And what is this woman's name?"

Crawford looked at his notes. "Anastasia Radcliffe. Her husband presumed she had drowned until knowledge of an item that once belonged to his late father-in-law was sold for cash in Topeka."

Jesse wasn't sure why, but the line of conversation began to bother him. "Why would that alert him to think otherwise?"

"Because the woman also sold the same jeweler some very fine and expensive pieces, most of which his wife was wearing the night she disappeared."

Jesse stroked his chin. Why was there that inkle of fear in the back of his throat? "We don't have anyone here by that name, Mr. Crawford. I'm sorry."

Again he went through his briefcase. "Well, perhaps if I show you a picture? It isn't very clear, but it was the only one the husband could find."

Jesse nodded, cautiously reaching for the sepia and studying it. His entire insides crumbled, and his hands shook. His face felt hot, and his eyes watered. He had to swallow his gorge to keep from vomiting. It was, indeed, Tansy Leigh. Or, as she was better known, Anastasia Radcliffe.

He forced a tight smile and handed the picture back, hoping the man didn't notice that his hands shook. "Sorry. She doesn't look familiar to me."

Clearly disillusioned, Mr. Crawford tucked the picture back into his briefcase. "Well, her husband will be very disappointed. She is an heiress to the Jarvis Mining Company. If I don't find her, it will be big news." He rose and took Jesse's hand.

"Sorry I couldn't help you out," Jesse said, watching the man leave.

She is an heiress to the Jarvis Mining Company. He slumped back into his chair and focused on something beyond the window, beyond the mountains, beyond the ocean. He was numb. He ached. His heart, his lungs, his head pounded with disbelief. He wanted to throw something. He wanted to rage through the streets, roaring like an animal. And perhaps for the first time in his life, he wanted to beat someone to a pulp with his goddamned fists.

And he remembered his thoughts about Tansy's change in attitude. That was it. She was just another socialite looking for a fling with a country sheriff.

Ellis Crawford was indeed disappointed. He was so certain this would be the end of the trail for the wayward wife. He walked to the boarding house to retrieve some things he left behind and hoped to catch one last glimpse of the woman who rented him the room. Handsome, she was. It was the first time he'd been attracted to a woman in a long time. Be that as it may, he wanted to catch the first train out. But what to tell his client?

As he took the steps to the porch, the door opened, and a woman came out. She was looking over her shoulder, talking to someone inside, and didn't see him. She bumped right into him.

"Oh, I'm sorry," she apologized with a smile. "I should watch where I'm going, shouldn't I?"

He got a good look at her and did a double take. She was tall, striking and had a head full of untamed dark ringlets. Excitement curled up his spine. By God, it was her! Same hair, same cleft in her chin, and although she certainly didn't look like a debutante, he was certain it was her. He had to force himself not to say something to her, for he remembered his client's wish to apprehend her himself.

As long as he got paid, he didn't care. But he did know for certain that the woman who passed him was the wayward wife.

He questioned why the sheriff had said he didn't recognize her. But he really didn't care about that. He had to get to a telegraph office quickly and send his message. And then he would get paid. And then what? How long could he keep chasing people all over the continent? It was actually getting tiresome.

Tansy felt terrible. She didn't have a fever. She didn't have a cough. And she wasn't coming down with the influenza. But she was still nauseous. In fact, when she got up to prepare for the day, she immediately felt like she was going to faint and had to go back to bed.

She was still resting when there was a knock on the door, and

Margot poked her head around, clearly alarmed when she saw Tansy in bed.

"Are you all right, honey?"

Tansy swallowed. "No. I still feel awful, Margot. I'm so sorry. Can you tell Gracie Jane I won't be able to be with her today?"

Margot waved away the question. "The sheriff has already left for the cabin with Gracie Jane."

That comment puzzled her. "I didn't realize they were going back. Was something wrong with Gracie Jane?"

"No, he said something about having to do some work. Cutting lumber or some such thing."

Tansy rolled over in bed. "It's just as well. I've been feeling this way for a while now."

Margot studied her, her arms crossed over her chest. "Huh. If I didn't know better, I'd think you were with child, but of course we all know that can't be."

Tansy gave her a weak smile and pulled the covers over her head. After Margot left, Tansy wondered. Could it be? Could she be carrying Jesse's baby? She guessed it was possible, but why, after a year of marriage, didn't she become pregnant before this?

And if she was, God help her, what would she do about it?

CHAPTER 21

*B*ear greeted them with his low, loud bark, his tail swishing from side to side as he met the carryall. Jesse deposited Gracie Jane in the cabin by the fire. There was a definite nip in the fall air. Of course, she had questioned why 'Miss Tansy' hadn't come with them, considering she was Gracie Jane's tutor, but Jesse made some excuse that seemed to satisfy his daughter.

Now he picked up the ax and took out his anger and frustration on splitting logs. He had to tell someone what he knew, or his head would burst. How to deal with it was another story.

He spent three hours splitting wood. When he was done there was a nice stash of it up against the lean-to wall. Although he was physically exhausted, his mind still whirled with newly found, very troubling information. But there would be enough wood for the winter, he was sure. He was still angry and frustrated, and yes, even hurt, goddammit. That made him even angrier.

That evening, after Gracie Jane went to sleep, Maybelle said, "Let's go out on the porch, Jesse." She picked up her knitting. Emmeline was already outside. Bear was lying at her feet.

He followed her to the porch. Jesse sat on the steps, and Maybelle took the other rocking chair.

"What's eating you, Jesse? I've known you all your life, and I know when something isn't right."

He scrubbed his face. "I hardly know where to start."

"The beginning is always nice." He heard the smile in her voice.

He dove right in. "Yesterday I learned who Tansy Leigh really is. Apparently, her husband hired a detective to find her."

"And he found her in Willow River? How can you be sure?"

Jesse looked out into the woods. Fireflies freckled the night sky. "He showed me a picture."

Maybelle inhaled sharply. "Oh, my. What did you tell him?"

Jesse pushed his sleeves up over his elbows. "I told him I didn't recognize her."

Her knitting needles clicked and clacked in the soft night air. "And why would you do that?"

He was quiet a moment, and then said, "At first it might have been because I didn't want to believe it. Her husband had abused her, she said. He physically beat her. Now I wonder if that was even the truth." He took out his tobacco pouch to roll a cigarette but changed his mind and stuffed it back into his pocket. "She told lie after lie from the very beginning. At this point I don't see any reason to believe her husband shouldn't come and haul her away from here."

Maybelle made a growling sound in her throat. "But what if he really did beat her? It wouldn't be safe for her to return."

"Right now I'm so angry I might just contact the man myself just to get her out of here."

"Oh, Jesse, you don't mean that." The knitting needles clicked and clacked.

"Tell us about her." Emmeline spoke. She had been silent up to now.

Jesse stood and paced the porch. He wouldn't beat around the bush. He'd tell it like it was and get it over with. "Her name is actually Anastasia Radcliffe. She's an heiress to the Jarvis Mining Company."

Maybelle sat in stunned silence. Her knitting fell to the floor. "The Jarvis—"

"Yeah, the same mining company that left my cousin, your son, to die."

Maybelle took a swift intake of air. "Jonah. That mine killed my Jonah."

"Oh, Jesse, surely you don't think she had anything to do with that. Why, that was fifteen years ago," Emmeline responded.

Jesse pressed his thumbs into his eyes. "I know, I know. But it's the connection... and the fact that she fled from massive wealth and comfort." He reached down and picked up Maybelle's knitting and put it on the small table beside her. "I know that she wouldn't leave all that on a lark. Her husband probably was violent. But that doesn't change the fact that she's a rich girl, does it?"

"You'd begun to care for her, hadn't you?"

"I suppose I had. Am I really so green that I could be taken in again?"

"Tansy, or whatever her name is, doesn't seem anything like Judith, Jesse. And I don't believe all rich people look down on the rest of us. Tansy certainly didn't. She appeared to actually enjoy being out here. Isn't that the impression you got, May?"

"Indeed. Remember how she looked in the fishing gear and waders?" Maybelle chuckled softly. "I don't think many high society types would be caught dead in such clothing, but your Tansy was comfortable as anyone in it."

"She's not my Tansy," Jesse mumbled, remembering how she'd followed him down to the beach in those damn waders. She didn't seem to have any fear. No woman he knew would have risked her safety as she had that night. And how deftly Tansy had climbed the tree to his old tree house. As if she'd done such things all her life as she claimed she had.

"Well," Em began, "I know you're probably angry and hurt, Jesse. You have reason to be. It doesn't do our self-image much good to learn we've been taken for a ride, especially by someone we've grown to care for and trust."

"But then again," May added, "she came here innocently, I believe. All of these coincidences are just that...coincidences. And not very pleasant ones, mind you. But I have good instincts, and I trusted her. I still do. Events have occurred that were not under her control."

Jesse shook his head. "And to think I was positive she wasn't a debutante. She's nothing like Judith. Nothing at all. And I wanted to believe she was just your ordinary woman, on the lam from a violent husband."

"Well, that part is probably true, Jesse."

Yeah, he thought, but she was anything but ordinary. He didn't want to believe she had purposely duped him. Yes, he was hurt and angry and wanted to punch holes in the jail walls, but after a while, after cutting wood for a few hours and some home spun logic from his aunts, he knew she wasn't any of the things Judith was.

"I'd like to stay for a while, kind of process everything, if you don't mind. I won't be very good company, but I'll try to stay out of your hair. Gracie Jane always loves it here."

"Don't you think Tansy will wonder why you left so quickly?" Maybelle picked up her knitting and began again. Click. Clack. Click.

Jesse had considered that. "She may wonder, but if she asks anyone, I've just come up here with Gracie Jane to do some of your harder work."

"Won't she wonder why you didn't invite her along?"

"I don't know. I don't know." But he did know that something was eating at Tansy for she indeed had become distant. Maybe it was all for the best.

Em went inside, Bear following. "We'd love it if you stayed forever, Jesse."

So would he. How great it would be to stay here with Gracie Jane and forget the world that waited for him in town. After Judith's surprise arrival, he realized he needed to keep Gracie Jane particularly safe. This was the place to do that, but he also knew none of them could escape reality forever. In a few days he would return to town, and he hoped he didn't meet Tansy Leigh, or Anastasia Radcliffe, when he did. But he knew that was unlikely.

As Oliver boarded the train for California, the telegram was stamped on his brain. *Wife in Willow River, California. Bypass the sheriff; go directly to the boarding house.* He only wished there was a faster way to get there.

One day Davey Pine showed up when Tansy was in the parlor, playing dismal dirges on the piano that matched her mood. She stopped playing and smiled at him.

He stepped from one foot to the other, clearly upset. Of course, losing his papa must have taken quite a bit of joy out of the boy. "I got somethin' to say, and since the sheriff ain't here, I'll tell you. Just not my ma."

She swung around on the piano stool. "What is it, Davey?"

He appeared to have difficulty finding his words. "Pa died…" He swallowed hard and wiped his eyes with the back of his hand. "I've been punished for doin' things, and I'm thinkin' that's why Pa died. Because of me."

She gave him a warm, sympathetic smile. "What things, Davey?"

He drew in a deep breath, as if about to confess the worst crime in the world. "I took your cape and gave it to my ma."

Her smile was genuine. "I know."

"But it's stealin'. I know that. I've taken other stuff that I knew belonged to someone else too."

"Have you kept it?"

"I woulda, but the sheriff made me give it all back."

"I don't think the world works like that, Davey. Your pa died because he had an infection in his lungs. It had absolutely nothing to do with you or what you've done in the past."

"Well, I ain't gonna take things no more, and I'll tell Ma to give you your cape."

"No. Don't do that. Actually, it looks quite nice on her, don't you think? And," she fabricated, "I have another I can use, so let's not upset your ma."

His eyes were shiny as he smiled his gape toothed smile.

"Thanks, Miss Tansy. I promise to be good, and I'll clean the jail real good too. The sheriff asked me to do that."

Ah, yes, Tansy thought. The sheriff. It had been days since she'd seen him. She did wonder why he stayed away so long, but perhaps it was for the best. Her heart didn't believe a word of it.

On his way out, Davey met his mother. "Bye, Ma. Gotta get to school."

Margot watched him go, a proud expression on her pretty face. "He's pretending to take his pa's death very well."

"I think he'll be just fine, Margot." She saw something in Margot's hands. "What do you have there?"

"It's a handkerchief. I found it in the room I rented to that nice Mr. Crawford. Guess he must have forgotten it."

"Crawford?"

"Oh, that's right, dear. You were ailing when he came for a room. And he only stayed the one night."

Tansy felt immediate guilt. "I'm sorry you've had to work so hard. I'm feeling much better now, and I can pull my weight around here."

"Well, you don't look as peaky as you did a few days ago. I put Ruta to work cleaning the vegetables for dinner. She says she's right as rain." She looked down at the handkerchief. "Guess I'll toss this in the laundry, just in case he comes back."

Tansy was anxious to freshen up. She was taking Gracie Jane on a late afternoon picnic. As she washed her face and changed into a worn but summery frock, she smiled a little sadly to herself. The only thing that would make it better would be if Jesse would join them. But when he dropped his daughter off at the rooming house, he simply waved at Tansy and went on his way. It was as if he couldn't get away from her fast enough.

Zeb positioned the wheelchair under the shade of an oak tree, promising to return in an hour.

Tansy thanked him, giving him a friendly hug before he went

on his way. "I can't thank you enough for being such a good friend," she said as she stepped away.

"All I know is that he's a good man and you are a good woman, and I believe the two of you belong together." He gave her shoulder a squeeze and left her and Gracie Jane alone.

"Did you get much reading done at the cabin?" She went about fishing food out of the basket. Everything smelled incredible, and she was starving. Fried chicken, biscuits, coleslaw, and ginger cookies. Tansy's mouth watered.

"We finished *Little Women*," Gracie Jane said sadly. "I'm going to miss them." She paused and picked at the grosgrain ribbon on her frock. "Especially Beth." She reached into the pocket in her chair and pulled out another ribbon, much shabbier and dirty. "Pesky left me this. I'll bet it was real pretty once. I still miss…"

Tansy fixed Gracie Jane a plate of lunch and put it on her lap. "What. What do you miss, Gracie Jane?"

Gracie Jane just looked at the food, listless. She gave Tansy a sad look. "Nothing is the same as it was. I wish we could go back."

"Back to what?" Tansy took a bite of chicken, savoring the taste.

"Back to the first time you came to the cabin with us. Papa was suddenly happier. He talked about you, you know, when you weren't around."

Her heart jumped in her chest. "He did, did he?"

"He told me how you climbed the tree where his tree house was and how you seemed so happy to be in the place that made him the happiest…"

Tansy unconsciously touched her stomach, wishing, again, for a miracle. "Things don't always turn out the way we want them, sweetheart."

"But why not? I know Papa likes you, and you like him, so why can't we just go on the way we were before?"

Tansy went to the wheelchair and put her arms around Gracie Jane's tiny shoulders. "Miracles don't always happen when we need them." She looked at the child's untouched lunch. "You should eat something, dear."

Gracie Jane picked up the cookie. "Well, maybe this."

Tansy bit the inside of her cheek to stop a smile. "A bite of chicken before you eat that, all right?"

And it was at this moment, with Gracie Jane's sad expression, that Tansy felt her lowest. Her situation with Jesse, her newly discovered pregnancy, her guilt at being someone she knew Jesse couldn't be proud of—all of these things made her feel worse than she had when Oliver hit her.

He watched from the bushes. His traitorous wife. And the man? Who was the man? Someone new in her life?

Anger and rage churned in his gut. For some reason, he hadn't thought about that possibility. That fed his rage. Not only was she a scheming bitch she was clearly unfaithful to her vows. It was another nail that could be pounded into her coffin. He clenched and unclenched his fists, wanting in the worst way to shove them into her face.

But for his plan to work, he could not. She must appear without blemish when he hauled her in front of the judge. Then again, he could say she got violent, and he had to calm her down. Yes, that would be better. He couldn't contain himself for an entire trip half way across the country.

He stealthily moved away toward the empty little hovel he'd found when he entered this cow pie town. The time was ripe. He was ready.

That evening, despite her mood, she sat at the piano and played Stephen Foster for the boys. When everyone else had gone to bed, she straightened up the parlor, stacking the music on top of the piano.

She was thinking of Walt, and how he sang his heart out to

every song, even though he couldn't carry a tune in a wash tub. And Oscar, for the first time, stood at the piano and sang merrily. Smiling at the memory, she began humming "Oh, Susanna."

"Good evening, Anastasia."

For just a moment, shock debilitated her. There was a movement in her chest, something plummeting heavily into her stomach. The reality that he'd actually found her hit her like a punch to the abdomen. She felt like she would vomit. She turned slowly and faced him.

He had not changed. Why would she think he would have changed? Although it had been mere months since she left, it felt like a lifetime. She swallowed repeatedly but couldn't find her voice.

Oliver studied her, his expression one of distaste. "You're living like a common wench. Have you lost your mind?" He glanced around the room. "Is this supposed to pass for a parlor? It's a seedy dump. Surely you must have lost your senses, Anastasia. Why else would you be living like this? Now gather your things, if you have anything worth taking, and come with me. Now. Or else."

Or else, what? You're going to beat me into submission? She wanted to say it, but she still couldn't speak.

She looked around...helpless. She was alone. With the man she detested and also feared. With the man who, apparently, would go to great lengths to find her and do what? She shuddered to think of the possibilities.

Seeing no way out for the moment, she held her head high and went to retrieve her things. With her heart heavy in her chest, she prayed for someone to come along, anyone, who might foil his plans.

Her prayer was not answered.

CHAPTER 22

The following morning, as Jesse rode from the cabin to the jail, he met the mail stage and took the sack of mail with him, promising to get everything delivered.

"Sorry it's late," the driver said. "The pass just opened up after that freak blizzard we had a few weeks back."

Jesse thanked him and went to the jail and heaved the sack on the desk. Lloyd came in and Jesse said, "Why don't you go through the mail? See that it's delivered, will you?"

Lloyd nodded, sat down at the desk, and dumped out the sack. A smattering of letters drifted to the desktop. He went through them one by one. "Hey, here's one for Miss Tansy."

"You should probably get it over to the boarding house. I'll look over the rest of it." He wasn't anxious to see her. Not yet.

It wasn't long before Lloyd was back, his expression clearly puzzled.

"What's wrong?"

"Miss Tansy ain't at the boarding house."

"She's probably down at the river, fishing or swimming," he said with a dry smile as he stacked the remainder of the mail on his desk.

Lloyd stepped from one foot to the other. "Well, no one has seen her at all today. She didn't come down for breakfast, and she wasn't around to help Margot with the laundry."

He retrieved his journal from the desk drawer. He wanted to record more raven activity before he forgot the details. "She'll show up. Did you leave the letter with someone?"

"I gave it to Ruta who was mighty curious about the contents."

"Hopefully she won't steam it open," Jesse answered, although he knew that's something she had done in the past.

Tansy sat stiffly on the bench seat of the train and kept her face toward the window, away from Oliver. They hadn't been alone yet, except at the house, and had he hit her then, someone would have heard it, for she would have cried out. Now they were on the train with other passengers, and she was grateful he couldn't hit her here either.

But he would. Yes, he would. Her husband would enjoy it too. And somehow, she would protect herself, for she knew now, so many weeks later, that she was pregnant with another man's child. She thought she'd hit a low point the other day. This was by far the lowest.

"Have you any idea what the bloody hell you've put us through?" His British accent slipped into something far less highborn sounding.

His words were said casually, but she knew him and knew he was livid. Sometimes, when he was very angry like now, his upper-class British accent slipped and became a bit vulgar and unpleasant. It was at those times she wondered if he was everything he'd said he was. She'd been to London. At times her husband sounded like every hawker and peddler in Trafalgar Square.

"Do you know where we're going?" he asked.

Still, she said nothing.

"You're not interested?" he said when she didn't answer. "You may bloody well be when we get there," he added. "How does going home to Chicago sound? There's a lovely place I've picked out just for you. Cook County has all the proper amenities for faithless wives." He sighed and settled himself deeper into the uncomfortable bench. "I'm tending toward electroconvulsive shock therapy. Or maybe insulin therapy. Do you know what that is? No? Well," he continued conversationally, "they inject you with insulin until you go into a coma and then, hopefully, when you come out of the coma, you're cured. However, I have a feeling you might not live through that. And believe me, faithless whore, I want you to live." His voice was a guttural hiss.

She tried to tune him out. She let her mind go back to California, to the ocean, the redwoods, to all of the beauty she had discovered since her arrival. The thrilling, albeit frightening experience she had when she was in the woods with Bear, and they encountered...something dangerous. Oh, it broke her heart that she wouldn't see the ocean again or smell the pungent salt air. Like the pine needles baking in the sun, the smell of the briny ocean water soothed her soul. Would there ever be anything again that would do that? And the shore birds pecking away at the sand, finding lunch. She hadn't gotten to walk along the beach to gather seashells or the perfect stone or watch the crabs sidle along in the tide pools.

Heartbreak was also knowing that she would never see it from Jesse's childhood tree house ever again. The idea of Gracie Jane growing up without her was more painful that she'd ever imagined. But she was grateful that everyone was aware of Gracie Jane's medical condition. Someone would continue to see that her joints didn't stiffen, and her patchy sores were soothed with balms. Now, she would never see her again. Whatever Oliver did to her, no matter what pain he inflicted, would never be as painful as not seeing Gracie Jane again. Not even being able to say goodbye. What would she think of her, skulking away in the middle of the night?

She would miss Ruta's bawdy speech and Davey's boyish grin and sticky fingers. And Will and Walt, brothers, peas in a pod, who never seemed dissatisfied with life. They had made her smile every day. And Zeb...the shell of a man that had once been powerful and productive. And even Oscar, whom she barely knew, but who had often helped her shake rugs and hang laundry. Such a funny little man. He probably weighed half of what she did.

But most of all, there was Jesse. She would miss him more than she could ever explain, but, she thought, running a hand over her stomach, a part of him would always be with her. Somehow. Some way. She had to believe that, or the rest of her life wouldn't be worth living.

Oliver's voice was intrusive, grating on her nerves, making it hard to concentrate. She hadn't eaten since the night he arrived, and her stomach growled. Could she stand his droning for the length of the journey? Dare she try to escape?

"Maybe a lobotomy," he continued. "But then, you might forget what you've put me through, and I won't allow that. No. I will not allow you to forget what a fool you have made of me and your entire family! Consider your very own mother. She wept when you 'died' and was even angry when I told her you were alive."

Tansy clamped her mouth shut. She wouldn't give him the satisfaction of asking why her mother was angry she hadn't died. But she could guess, and it probably had more to do with what people would think than with Tansy herself.

"Indeed, your mother and I believe you have lost your mind. Perhaps hysteria. Maybe even melancholia. We all knew how much you missed your pompous ass of a father. We agree that you would not have left your luxurious lifestyle had you not had some serious brain event."

He stopped then, as if wanting her to process everything he had just told her. And she did. With two important people in her life to consider her crazy, did she have a chance at all of coming out of this unscathed? The future looked so very bleak. How could she escape it?

The door to the office swung open, hitting the wall with a bang. "Jesse!" Ruta came in, red-faced and breathless.

"What's wrong?"

"What's wrong? Everything's wrong! Tansy is gone."

Oh, that again. "Like I told Lloyd, she's probably at the river."

Ruta's fist came down hard on the desk. "She. Is. Gone."

He leaned back, taking in Ruta's obvious distress. "What makes you think so?"

"I took the letter up to her room and when she didn't answer, I opened the door and went in." She took a deep breath and patted the place over her heart. "Jesse, her things are gone. Her beat up old satchel…everything."

Now he was interested and began to feel uneasy. Had she just up and left? "She didn't say anything to anyone?"

Ruta was still out of breath. "Last night she played for the fellers like always. That's the last anyone saw her."

"Where's the letter?"

She plucked it from her apron pocket and handed it to him. "You open it. You're the law. You can do that."

He looked at the writing. It was probably from her sister. "All right, I will. But I don't really think it's a good idea."

Ruta motioned for him to get on with it.

He opened it and read the few lines written there, and his heart did a somersault in his chest. *Oliver knows you're alive. A detective is on the way. Flee!* Without speaking, he handed the missive to Ruta, who took it, read it, and gasped.

"But she hadn't gotten this message yet, so why is she gone?"

That, Jesse realized, fear climbing his ribcage, was a very good question. The detective had been here. Had he somehow kidnapped Tansy?

He strode to the door and lifted his hat off the peg. Before leaving, he said to Ruta, "I'll make some inquiries. Find out if the detective spent more than a night at the boarding house. Maybe he stuck around somewhere else, waiting until he could grab her."

"He didn't," Ruta answered. "There was a train at six. He told Margot he was going to take it. And she saw him get on."

"I'll check it out."

An hour later, all Jesse knew was that the detective had, indeed, left on the evening train, alone. And anyway, that was a week ago. He steepled his fingers over his lips and tried to think of every imaginable reason Tansy could be gone without telling anyone.

He supposed she could have left, knowing what he knew now, also knowing that he knew about the connection to the Jarvis Mines. He didn't like to think she'd simply up and leave without at least saying something to Gracie Jane. And she had not.

He would contact Tansy's sister. Hopefully she knew something he didn't.

They got off the train one night, and Oliver booked a hotel room so he could get a good night's sleep. Tansy knew she would not sleep a wink, especially with her wrist handcuffed to the bedpost so she wouldn't attempt escape.

And he had warned her not to call for help. "It would be fruitless. All I have to do is tell them you're irrational, and anything you say is simply crazy talk. And believe me, bitch, the more you tried to convince someone otherwise, the more frustrated you would become, proving my point."

She lay there, fully clothed as Oliver primped into a mirror over the dry sink. When he'd finished, he walked to the bed and checked the handcuffs.

He gave her a wily smile. "Don't want you getting away while I'm gone." He checked himself in the mirror once more and then left her.

She pulled against the handcuffs repeatedly and finally realized there was no way she could get free. She did fall asleep and had no idea how long she'd slept, but suddenly Oliver was over her, gazing down as he removed his coat, his shirt, and his trousers.

The moonlight streaming into the room allowed her to see him clearly. He wore expensive garters to keep his hose from slipping. Did men ever wonder how ridiculous they looked in them? His legs were pale and hairless. She looked away.

"What's on your mind, faithless wife?"

She studied the door that led to the hallway outside the hotel room.

"I could have just let you go," he mused, crawling in beside her. The bed sagged as he settled into it. "But in order to inherit, I do believe you must be either dead or committed."

She scooted as far from him as she could, considering her restriction.

He laughed, and it was not a pleasant sound. "Relax, my unfaithful bitch, I don't want your unappealing body nor will I hit you. However," he added, "perhaps a bruise would be timely for I could say you tried my patience and deserved it. Who would believe otherwise?"

And she had thought any bruise he left on her would be a mark against him. How foolish of her to think it. She could well be bruised and bloody, and Oliver's answers to any questions would be reasonable. She still wondered why he hadn't laid a hand on her. And Tansy had no reason to believe she was going anywhere but an asylum.

Before he went to sleep, he turned to her and said, "If nothing else, I can prove you've been unfaithful to me."

Shock washed through her, but still she said nothing.

"I saw you with your scraggly paramour," he said with a sneer in his voice.

Fear continued to climb her chest.

"He's rather a bedraggled individual, wouldn't you say? Skinny as a bean pole and needing a good shave." He snorted. "I would have thought you might have better taste than that, but I was wrong. And your little picnic. Was that his crippled brat in the wheelchair? You can't do much screwing around with a kid looking on, can you?"

Tansy closed her eyes and exhaled. He had seen them at the picnic and assumed Zeb was her beau. She almost laughed but held it back, else it would have come out as hysteria, proving him right.

Sleep was not possible. As she lay there, she twisted her wrist and heard a soft popping sound. She almost gasped aloud, for the cuff that had been circling her wrist had opened!

Attempting to steady her breathing, she glanced over at Oliver, who was on his back, snoring loudly. She swallowed the lump of fear in her throat and eased slowly and carefully off the bed. She stood for a long moment, waiting to make certain her husband did not waken.

Then, with nothing more than the clothes on her back, she slipped out the door and was gone.

In Atlanta, Sally and Jacob Halloran stared at the telegram. Sally's hands trembled. She couldn't hold onto it, and it drifted to the top of the desk.

It was from the sheriff in Willow River, explaining Tansy's disappearance and wondering if there was something they should know, or something they could do.

"So the detective found her, but didn't bring her back with him? That seems odd," Sally said.

Jacob, far more pragmatic and methodical than his wife, could only make a conjecture. "Knowing Oliver as we now do, what if he wanted to approach her himself? Doesn't that sound like something a sadist would do? Frighten the wits out of her and make her fear for her life?"

Sally brought her hands to her face. "If that's what happened, she's in real trouble, Jacob. Remember what Mama said about Anastasia? That both she and Oliver wondered if she had lost her mind? What if...what if he takes her directly to the asylum without any of us knowing? We'd never get her out of there." She paused and bit at her bottom lip. "And if that's what he's doing, we don't even know which miserable place it will be."

"I think you're getting ahead of yourself, sweetheart." But Jacob didn't sound that convinced.

Sally disagreed. "What else could he do? No, we have to let the sheriff know Oliver's plans for her. I don't know what he can do about it, but in the meantime, you and I must have a plan ourselves."

He leaned back in his chair and gazed at her, his eyes filled with warmth and in spite of the situation, even a little mirth. "What do you propose we do?"

Sally began pacing the library, the hem of her skirt swishing as she walked. Part of her meticulous honey colored bun had come loose, and long strands of silky hair hung down her back. She strode to the door, turned and walked to the window. She studied the lawn for a moment, and then quickly twirled back and pinned her husband with a poignant look.

"Remember in Anastasia's letter, she said her maid, Clarice, was the only one who ever saw what Oliver did to her?" When Jacob nodded, she continued. "Suppose we find her and see if she would willingly stand up in court and report what she saw?"

"Fine idea, but I'm not sure the words of a servant girl would carry much weight in the courtroom."

"But isn't it worth a try?" She gave him one of her prettiest looks, one she had used in the past to get what she wanted from her wonderful husband.

His expression told her he knew what she was trying to do. "I suppose it's worth a try. But first, let's answer this telegram."

CHAPTER 23

*J*esse paced. Until he heard from Tansy's sister, he didn't know what to do with himself. That morning Zeb had offered his services in case Tansy needed a lawyer. Jesse knew that if she needed one, her brother-in-law would be available, but knowing how good Zeb was in his prime, he thanked him and asked him, if he could, to stay off the booze until they knew for sure.

Time would tell if Zeb could do that, but he told Jesse he would try. For Tansy, he would really try.

When the telegram finally came, Jesse whipped it from the stationmaster's hand and read it.

Husband took Anastasia plans to institutionalize her on basis of hysteria, mental illness or melancholia have started checking hospitals in area
Jacob Halloran

Jesse crumpled the note in his fist. Now what? So the bastard came into town, right to the boarding house, and no one saw him. How could this happen? The man was right under his nose, and he saw nothing. Tansy must have been scared to death when she realized her husband had found her.

Jesse had never felt more helpless in his life. But he did know

181

one thing—he would find out where they were going. They didn't have that much of a head start. If he hurried, he could get Lloyd settled into the job, pack a bag, and be on the next train out of town.

Sally had wasted no time preparing to leave for Chicago. The train ride was despicable, but she barely noticed, for every thought in her head was focused on finding her sister before it was too late.

After learning where Clarice was now employed, Sally took a cab to the address. Now, as she waited in the foyer for Clarice, she felt stronger than ever that the girl could be just what they needed to help her sister.

"Ma'am?"

Sally swung around. Clarice stood in the doorway to the rest of the house, her hands clasped tightly in front of her and a questioning look on her pretty, unlined face. She wore a drab brown day dress with a white apron over it.

Sally went to her immediately and took her hands in her own. "Oh, Clarice. Is there somewhere we can talk?"

Clarice glanced about, still concerned, for Sally's presence obviously puzzled her. "Come with me. To my room. I...I'm sorry it's so small."

Sally waved away her concern but understood it. The room was a small cubicle behind the fireplace in the kitchen barely big enough for one person, certainly not comfortable for two. They sat together on the bed.

"What is it, ma'am? Have I done something wrong?"

"Oh, Clarice, no, no nothing like that. I know this is going to be a shock to you, but...but I have to tell you that Anastasia didn't drown."

Puzzled, Clarice just looked at her.

"In fact, she didn't die, Clarice. She's alive."

Clarice could barely contain her relief and disbelief. She put her face in her hands and wept.

Sally told her all that had happened, the missing jewelry found in Topeka, the detective who discovered Anastasia in California, and Oliver's mission to put his wife away forever.

Clarice sat in awe. "She's alive. Oh, ma'am, I'm so happy she's alive! She didn't drown?"

Sally shook her head. "She didn't drown." She gave the girl a private look. "You wouldn't happen to know why she would fake her death, do you?"

"Oh, no ma'am. I wouldn't know anything about that. But she was the nicest person to me." She glanced around her closet-like room. "No one has ever treated me like she did." She hung her head, as if embarrassed, and added, "It was almost like we were friends."

"And you, Clarice, happen to be the only person who ever saw what Oliver did to her," Sally went on.

Clarice's eyes got big. "Yes, yes, I saw every single thing. I saw all the bruises, the bumps, the cuts, the welts..." She pressed her lips together. "He was so terribly mean to her. So terribly mean. I was glad when he let me go. I couldn't have stayed to work for him with Miss Anastasia gone." She blinked repeatedly. "Are you saying she left because of what he did to her?"

"I got a letter from her, Clarice. At the time I didn't know where she was, but I knew she was all right. She told me all about the beatings she received from Oliver and all the humiliations. Not long after that I learned that Oliver had hired the detective to find her. I wrote to warn her, but something must have happened to the letter, because Oliver... found her."

Clarice wiped her face with the back of her hand. "Oh, my. What will he do to her?"

"Oliver told my mother that he will put her in an asylum."

Clarice gasped and covered her mouth with her hand.

Sally shifted, uncomfortable. "Clarice, I have something to ask you, and I want you to think carefully before you answer."

Perplexed, Clarice said, "I don't understand."

"There are a lot of legal issues, but to put it plainly, we believe Oliver is going to have Anastasia committed to an asylum, claiming hysteria or melancholia, so he can inherit all of her assets."

"Melancholia?"

"It's when a person suffers greatly after the death of a loved one, in this case, our father."

"But, she—"

"I know," Sally interrupted. "She grieved as we both did, but she was closer to him than I was. Oliver could make a case by telling the judge just how close her bond was with Papa, and this is why she 'lost her mind' and left."

Clarice gasped. "But...that's...that's not right." She turned and faced Sally. "The night she left, she hugged me. She had never done that before, don't you see? She must have planned to leave. Why else would she have worn so much jewelry? She hated most of it. Anything from Mister Oliver repulsed her so much she didn't even want to touch it. But then I saw her put a bracelet he'd given her in her pocket that night, and she looked at me and put a finger to her lips.

"Both her husband and her mother grilled me over and over again, but I never told them. I never did. He even ridiculed her for wearing that big diamond. I...I remember him saying if it were up to him, he'd sell it. And do you know what she said? She said, 'well, it isn't up to you, is it?'"

Sally was amazed at Clarice's long critique, but asked, "Why is that unusual?"

"Because she never talked back to him. She knew what would happen if she did."

"And you think that because she was planning her escape, she said something that she wouldn't have said otherwise?"

"Exactly."

Sally considered everything that had been said and made her decision. "Clarice, would you be willing to stand up in court and tell a judge what you observed during your tenure as my sister's maid?"

"Me?" she squeaked. "Why would anyone believe me? I'm just a servant."

"But you're the only one who knows firsthand what he did to her."

Many emotions flitted over Clarice's face: fear, uncertainty, anger and finally resolve. "I will do anything to keep Miss Anastasia from such a terrible fate."

Jacob Halloran was reading the newspaper when his older daughter, Mamie entered the library. He glanced up and found her looking at him curiously.

"What is it, Mamie?"

She held a book in her hand, and a piece of paper. "Papa, I picked up one of Aunty Anastasia's books to read, and I found this paper tucked between the pages." It hadn't been opened yet. Jacob noted that the book was *Little Women*.

She handed the paper to her father, who opened it and what he read stunned him. But should he have been? Jacob stood and paced the library, his thoughts whirling. What did this mean and how could they use this information to their advantage?

Clearly his father-in-law had meant for Anastasia to read this before her marriage.

There must be some way to contact Scotland Yard to alert them of Oliver's whereabouts.

Jacob wasn't sure if the letter was enough evidence to put a stop to Oliver or if they needed proof from London to do so.

He threw on his overcoat, told the maid he was leaving for a while, and raced to the telegraph office.

Tansy ran wildly. She had no plan. She just wanted to get as far away from Oliver as possible.

It was dark. A few lamps were lit along the sidewalk, spilling out meager amounts of light as she ran past the shadowy buildings. She stumbled over a wooden step, righted herself, hiked her skirt up, and ran on, having no idea where she was going.

A light in a window up ahead drew her, and she raced toward it. She banged on the door with her fist, her breath clutching her lungs. "Please! Help me, please!"

It opened, and a woman stood there, dressed in an expensive looking robe, belted tightly around her small waist. Tansy barely noticed anything else. "Oh, thank god," she said around a wavering sigh. "Please, I…I don't know what you can do for me, but can you let me stay here for a bit?"

The woman opened the door wide and let her in. Tansy nearly staggered as she crossed the threshold but held on to the door jamb and had her first look around the room. It was pleasant and rather expensively furnished. Tansy collapsed onto the sofa, rested her head against the back, closed her eyes, and attempted to catch her breath.

When she opened them, the woman was sitting next to her with a glass of something in her hand. "Here," she said. "It's brandy. It'll calm you down." After a moment, she asked, "What's happened? What are you running from?"

Reluctant to tell a total stranger her story, she merely fabricated one. She had become good at that. She took a sip of brandy, which she'd had before, and allowed the heat to burn a path down her throat. "I was…on the train and was accosted by a total stranger," she began. "I got off here. I don't even know where we are, but I hid for a while in the baggage area, and then, as they began removing the baggage, I fled."

She finally looked at her hostess. Tall, thin, with vibrant red hair, she had a confident air about her. And she was quite attractive. Suddenly, aware that she may have interrupted something, she asked, "Am I intruding?"

The woman gave her a warm smile. "Of course not. Listen," she said as she rose from the couch. "Why don't you rest here for a bit? You look exhausted. If you plan to re-board the train, you'll have to wait until morning anyway. And here," she added, "drink this down. It will help you rest."

The brandy worked quickly and before she had a chance to

reconsider, she was asleep. During that time, she woke often, willing herself to move, but she always found it too difficult and let herself be swept back into slumber.

Finally, as dawn streamed in through the window, Tansy woke up, feeling a bit groggy, but able to function. She sat up and swung her legs off the sofa. Glancing across the room, she saw someone sitting in the chair by the small fireplace.

"Good morning, faithless bitch."

$\mathcal{F}$or Jesse, the train couldn't go fast enough. He had learned that Oliver's tickets had been paid through to Chicago, leaving a pretty obvious trail. He had sent a telegram to Tansy's brother-in-law with that news. Maybe he could track them down from there.

He wasn't sure just what he would do when he got there, but he had let the brother-in-law know where he could reach him should everything come together. Zeb had suggested a gentleman's club. Despite the sound of it, he assured Jesse it was not a high-class establishment. Now, all Jesse could do was hope.

Gracie Jane was in good hands at the cabin, although she had cried when she heard he was leaving, but understood that in order to find Tansy, he had to go. She had looked up at him with those pleading velvet brown eyes and said, "Please, Papa, I miss her so." He hadn't the heart to tell her that Tansy was never coming back.

As the train rattled along, spewing coal dust and debris, Jesse turned his thoughts to Tansy. Tansy, the tall, well-endowed, statuesque dark-haired beauty who had claimed his heart. Tansy, the woman with the infectious laugh, a woman who could swim and fish and climb like any man he'd known. Tansy, who had done every task asked of her even though she'd never done them before. Tansy Leigh: Anastasia Radcliffe. Heiress to two fortunes.

A woman so far out of his league there was no way to straddle the chasm.

Jesse had no illusions. His motive was to make sure she was not mistreated by the lout of a husband. He knew there was no future for them. She had already begun pulling away from him before all of this happened.

Fortunately, there was her sister and brother-in-law, both of whom had Tansy's welfare foremost in their minds. In the meantime, once again, all he could do was hope.

Stay, jailor, stay, and hear my woe!
She is not made who kneels to thee,
For what I'm now, too well I know,
And what I was and what should be.
I'll rave no more in proud despair,
My language shall be mild though sad;
But yet I'll firmly, truly swear,
I am not mad, I am not mad!
My tyrant husband forged the tale
which chains me in this dismal cell;
my fate unknown my friends bewail –
Oh, jailer, haste that fate to tell!

From the Asylum Journal, 1842, by an anonymous woman inmate.

Tansy prepared herself for the worst. After Oliver had found her —to Tansy's dismay, she had stumbled into the home of the woman Oliver had spent the evening with—he wasted no time in making sure she suffered for her attempt to escape.

Now, as she watched him speak with the matron of the asylum, she gently touched her jaw, which still ached from his punch. She couldn't open her mouth wide as the pain was excruciating.

A big, husky woman with pale eyes and a stern manner

whisked her away. She was shoved into a large gallery, paint chipped and peeling off the walls. Beds lined the walls. She guessed perhaps eight or ten on each side. The smell nearly overwhelmed her. She took in the scene before her and had to keep her knees from buckling. There were signs of madness everywhere.

"What am I to do here?" She spoke the words quietly to herself and kept her panic at bay, but fear could be harvested from every nerve in her body.

The woman said nothing and left her standing there. She lumbered to the door, and Tansy heard the door lock with a clanking, echoing bang. It sounded so final…

As she further studied the room, she saw other ladies sitting in chairs, some in wheelchairs. One woman was tied to her chair, her head resting on her chest. Tansy covered her mouth when she saw the spittle rolling from between the woman's lips. Another was picking frantically at something on her sleeve that Tansy couldn't see. Swallowing hard, she joined another who was close to the window. Tansy looked outside. An iron grate met her gaze. To cover her own fears, she turned to the woman and said, "Well, I guess that's the end of my plan to escape out the window."

The woman rose and walked to the far side of the room.

But as the daylight became dimmer and night closed in, Tansy's own sense of forced mirth left her. She realized that *this* was the lowest point in her life. It certainly couldn't get much worse.

The smell. Sleep was impossible. The air was ripe with a suffocating stench. Tin vessels without lids or covers filled with every conceivable filth offered the answer. Tansy forced herself not to gag, but since she discovered she was pregnant her gag reflex had become more active.

The first night she clung to the window, her head pressed against the iron bars, so she could inhale fresh, cool air. She longed for her little room at the boarding house where the air was fresh and clean and simply "there" with no one to appreciate it now that she was gone. How frivolous humans were when it came to air. They used it without thought.

As days went by, something as free as fresh air became a commodity she couldn't buy or steal. She requested a bath. She was told it was not part of the plan. Plan, she thought? Did Oliver really mean to keep her in this miserable hole into hell and not allow her to bathe? But they cut off her hair, all of it. She watched as each dark ringlet hit the floor. Her hair had always been rather a nuisance, but seeing it thus made her sorry she ever disliked it. But she reminded herself, it was just hair; it would grow back. But not if she never left this place...

On the fourth day, Tansy, whose jaw still ached, believed her guardian angel had finally come to help, for, as matron told her, she was a 'big' girl and could handle trays of dishes so was allowed to work in the kitchen. No one seemed to notice that she had not bathed; no one really looked at her at all.

She realized that the help, everyone from the lowliest cleaning person (Tansy wondered what they cleaned. It seemed to her everything was filthy.) to the matron, her staff and the physicians, received good food. They often had meals which included fine wines and beef steaks and roasts. Fat cows grazed outside her window in a meadow filled with lush grass. Sometimes, as she pressed herself against the grate, even the grass looked good enough to eat, and her mouth would water.

But she dared not take any scraps. One older woman was seen slipping a beef bone into her apron pocket. Tansy heard later than she had been put into a hot bath, her head held under water, until she turned blue and fainted.

All this time, Tansy tried to eat what was put before her. Dry bread. Dry cheese. Watery gruel. Occasionally, on the worst days, her food would be crawling with something she didn't recognize and refused to try to identify. Knowing she was feeding her baby, she ate what she could, holding her breath, and closing her eyes as she swallowed it. Otherwise she put the pregnancy in the back of her mind. To wonder at her future was far too painful.

One day, as Tansy left the kitchen, another patient approached her, a woman dressed in drab gray clothing, as filthy as her own, whose countenance was as clear as a bright day near her beloved Pacific Ocean. Pacific: Peace. Thoughts of California were often the only things that kept her sane.

The woman touched Tansy's arm. "Don't be alarmed, I beg you," she whispered. Tansy slowed her pace, and they walked together yet did not appear to be together. "I know who you are," she murmured.

"I beg your pardon?" Tansy kept her voice low.

"You are Anastasia Radcliffe, are you not?"

Hesitantly, Tansy nodded. "Why have you approached me?"

"You don't remember me." The woman wasn't disappointed. It was merely a comment.

Tansy threw the woman a glance. "I'm sorry, I'm afraid I don't."

Suddenly they were both shoved from behind. One of the young assistants growled, "On your way, ladies. No loitering."

Tansy was pulled away from the other woman and propelled into her room, clearly puzzled yet quite excited at the prospect of someone to talk with.

A week went by before the woman found her alone again. Tansy had taken food scraps out to the pigs. The animals ate far better than the inmates. The aide who was to accompany her to make sure she didn't eat them herself had been called away. As Tansy approached the barn where the pigs were kept, she heard her name. The woman stood behind the door, hidden from view.

Tansy kept to her task as the woman spoke.

"Your mother and I once belonged to the same charity group," the woman said. "My name is Mary Clara Brooks. It doesn't matter if you don't remember me, but it's imperative that you listen to me."

The woman went on to explain how she came to be at the asylum, a story not so very different from Tansy's.

"I have always been strong willed," the woman told her. "That very will put me here, for my husband could no longer control me, or so I was told. But I vow to get my release, and when I do, I shall write down every abominable thing I have seen here."

Tansy perked up. "I'm interested," she said, wanting to hear more. Although she had no reason to believe she, herself, would ever be free again.

"With your connections, your voice would be a strong one to support what I will say," Mrs. Brooks claimed. "We may go before a judge, but the men in our lives control everything, and that was one reason I'm here. I voiced my opinion in front of not only my husband but one of his friends and embarrassed my husband."

Tansy tossed the last of the scraps, which smelled so delicious her mouth watered, and answered her. "If I ever get my release, which I truly doubt, I will support you with all of my heart. If you ever need funds, I will help you."

The woman thanked her and hurried away before she was seen, leaving Tansy to wonder if she, too, could even begin to think about freedom.

When her thoughts became darkest, Tansy often wondered what was happening in the world outside. Had Oliver convinced everyone that she was mad, or had he concocted another story, perhaps one that already had her dead by some accidental cause, this time her body never found.

What of the rest of her family? Because of Tansy's letter to her sister, both she and Jacob knew what Oliver had put her through. Would there be any way they would think to find out what happened to her?

And what of Jesse? Oh, dear Jesse. Her heart ached when she thought of him, and how he must have assumed she left him as Judith had. He would never know she carried his child. She beseeched her angel to keep the baby safe. She was helpless to do anything else.

Weeks ago, she had come to peace with the fact that everything she had brought with her was now gone. She had nothing save the clothes on her back and a pair of shoes so worn there were holes in the soles. She had the audacity to ask one of the assistants where her belongings had gone and was told, quite gruffly that there were others who needed her things because she no longer did. 'Others' meant the staff, Tansy was sure.

Everything was gone. Her meager clothing, her papa's satchel and her coins...or what was left of them.

She thought of her blue cashmere cape and was ecstatic—if ecstasy could even be acquired in this place—that Margot Pine wore it and not some fleshy, pasty matron or one of her lumbering, sadistic assistants.

At night, when she could no longer stand at the window to breathe, she lay down on her bed, turned on her side, and cradled her stomach, which, despite everything, was growing. She had felt the quickening and was so happy she nearly wept. She would whisper poetry she had learned as a girl and had never forgotten. She loved Poe's works, his grim, dismal view of life. For a girl who always looked on the positive side, she realized Poe was a poor choice. Annabel Lee was a favorite, perhaps on some unconscious level, she felt akin to the girl, for the stanza *So that her highborn kinsman came and bore her away from me, to shut her up in a sepulcher in this kingdom by the sea* was one she never forgot. Of course, Annabel Lee died. Tansy refused to believe that was in the stars for her.

CHAPTER 25

*T*ansy had been in the asylum over a month when the matron showed up at her bedside early one morning.

"Get up. You've got a visitor."

Startled, Tansy brought the grimy blanket to her chin and just stared at the woman.

The matron kicked the bed. "You lost your tongue or your hearing, girl? Get up. You've got a visitor."

Tansy scrambled from the cot, completely befuddled. "Who is it?" She found her voice. It croaked like a frog's.

"It isn't my duty to tell you. Get dressed. I'll be right outside the door. Now hurry it up."

Tansy's mind suddenly whirled. Oliver? Had Oliver changed his mind? Who else could it be? No one knew she was here. She pulled on her grubby gown, attempting to smooth the wrinkles. Nothing could be done about the dirt. She hurried to the door and followed the matron downstairs into the first room the patients saw when they entered. It was clean and well-appointed. Nothing like the rest of the place.

She stepped inside and looked for Oliver. The only person there was a woman who stood gazing into the fireplace. Suddenly the woman turned. "Anastasia?"

Tansy's entire body abandoned her. Her knees were gone, and she heard some kind of noise around her, but she didn't understand what it was. And then suddenly she knew. She was weeping so hard she was gagging on her own air. Her knees were so weak she had to cling to the sofa to stay upright. Her sister was beside her and helped her sit. And then Sally's arms were around her.

Tansy wanted her sister's touch, but she pulled away. "No, no, please don't touch me. I'm...I'm filthy, Sally. I have not been allowed to bathe, and I have no other cloth—"

Sally shushed her and held her tight. "Oh, my darling." Tears filled Sally's voice. "What has he done to you?"

"You know he did this?" Oh, her sister smelled so sweet! And her voice was a melody, rather melancholic, but still melodic to Tansy's ears.

"We all know." Sally leaned away. "I'll tell you everything, but first let's get you out of here."

Tansy gasped. "I...I can leave?"

Sally helped her to rise. "Right now. Jacob has filled out the proper papers, and he and Jesse are waiting outside."

Tansy stopped breathing, abruptly resisting Sally's urge to walk to the door. "Jesse is here?"

"As I said, I'll tell you everything once we're far from this place."

"But...but I can't see Jesse."

"Why on earth not?"

Tansy spread her arms. "Look at me, Sally. My dress is a rag, I'm practically bald, and I haven't bathed since I left California." There were dirty smudges everywhere, and although she couldn't smell herself, she knew she reeked. "He can't see me like this, Sally. He just can't."

Sally gave her a long, loving look. "My dear sister, no one cares what you look like. We're just happy to have you back."

Tansy shook her head. "I understand. But please, Sally, let me clean up first before I see...anyone else. I...it's just..." She couldn't seem to make her sister understand. All she knew was that she wouldn't see Jesse or anyone else until she'd had a bath. But the fact that he was here was puzzling to her as well.

Sally began to appreciate her sister's situation. With a sigh, she stood and went to the door. "All right, I'll fix it."

Jesse was climbing out of his skin. The process of getting Tansy out of this awful place was taking longer than he'd expected. But Jacob had promised him she would be out. He clung to that.

Sally stepped outside alone. His heart sank. She walked right up to him.

"What is it?" It didn't even sound like his voice.

"She doesn't want to see anyone until she's...ready."

"What in the hell does that mean?" He sounded defensive. He couldn't help it. "I know she doesn't expect me to be here, but I'm here, and I just want to know that she's all right."

"Jesse, she's all right, under the circumstances. I don't think any of us could possibly imagine what she has been through this past month." Sally glanced at her husband. "You two find another way to get to the hotel and give us some time. I'll take Anastasia there in the cab. Now get out of here, both of you."

Jesse followed Jacob to the street where they waited for a cab. Suddenly he said, "I think I'll walk back to the hotel, Jacob."

Jacob gave him a long look. "Suit yourself. I don't know what your relationship is with Anastasia, but—"

"We don't have a relationship," he said, hating the sound of the words. "She's someone who is very special to my daughter, and I need to know that she's all right before I return home."

Jacob clasped his hands behind his back. "You realize that she and Oliver were never legally married, don't you?"

"I've heard the whole sordid story. She's lucky to be rid of him. If I could have, I'd have done it myself."

Jacob's look was sly. "All because she's special to your daughter."

"Yes." The word came out harsh, and Jesse knew in his heart that there was so much more he wanted from her, but he knew what they'd had was over. "Regardless of what she's going through at this moment, she's home. Where she belongs." He almost added 'with her money and her social standing' but knew it would be wrong to say it. Tansy had not been like Judith. He doubted she was ever that self-absorbed, even living her luxurious lifestyle.

Jacob said, "Well, you have one thing right. She's home where she belongs, if, indeed, that's where she wants to be."

Jesse let the cryptic words slide over him as he turned and began walking the miles to the hotel. Actually, the longer he put off seeing her, the longer he could still think of her as once being his. Once they met again, face to face, his little fantasy would be over.

Tansy stepped into the hotel suite, stopped and simply stared. "Oh, my. I'd forgotten how beautiful things could be." Two large grey overstuffed chairs flanked a dark blue sofa. Everything was laden with cushions and pillows. The wallpaper was gilded with gold and pink and green flowers, with an enormous mirror over the white, ornate fireplace. She avoided it. No sense shocking her system any more by having to see what she looked like.

"Your bath is ready," Sally said, interrupting her thoughts.

Tansy walked to the bath and opened the door. "Clarice!"

Clarice, tears streaking her cheeks, came around the tub and grabbed Tansy's hands. "Oh, ma'am, I'm so happy to see you!"

Tansy's laughter mingled with tears. "Not like this, I hope."

"Here," Clarice began, "let me help you out of those clothes."

"Clarice, these are not clothes, these are rags." She stepped out of the clothing she had worn for a month and stepped into a tub of soapy water, scented with something fresh she couldn't place. She leaned against the back of the tub and sighed. In all of her life she had never appreciated a bath as she did at this moment.

"Oh, they cut off your hair!" Clarice's words jarred her a little. Loud voices and noises had a tendency to do that now.

"Just wash what's left of it, dear." And just like that, they were together again.

Clarice washed her back as she always did. Suddenly Tansy sat up and said, "I can do this myself now, can't I?" She still didn't know what happened to Oliver, but she realized that somehow, he was no longer a part of her life, for she had been told not to give him a thought.

She allowed Clarice to wash her hair, what was left of it, and as she stood to get out of the tub, Clarice gasped.

"Ma'am?"

Tansy noticed Clarice's gaze went to her stomach. She looked down and saw, for the first time, her rounded tummy. Her heart beat strong, and a joy that sent her senses tingling filler her. She put her hand over it, moving it around and around, sensing the life that was safely shielded there. "Ah, yes, the baby."

The alarm in Clarice's voice brought Sally into the bathroom. She stared at her sister a bit dumbfounded. "Anastasia? Do you have something to tell us?"

Feeling foolish, elated, embarrassed and relieved, Tansy said, "Isn't it obvious?"

Both women rushed to her side, toweled her off, and gave her a silk robe to slip into. Then they led her into the sitting room where a warm cup of tea and a feast of breakfast delights met her. She immediately sat down and began to eat. "Oh, my god," she murmured. "I'm starving." But knowing what she'd just been through, she tried to take things in slowly. The first bite of scrambled eggs melted in her mouth. The toast was hot and so slathered with butter it nearly ran down her chin. An anxious feeling hit her stomach, and she momentarily stopped to let it catch up to her greedy appetite.

Sally cleared her throat. "Anastasia?" She sat down next to her sister and rubbed her shoulders.

Tansy washed down a bite of buttered toast with a sip of tea, unaware of her sister's angst, her focus still on her ravenous appetite.

"Tansy!"

The urgency in her sister's voice startled her, and she realized both women were eager to hear how she got herself in this condition. No point beating around the bush. "The baby is Jesse Wolfe's."

Sally sat back, amazed. "Well, it's no wonder he's so anxious to find out how you are."

After a spoonful of strawberries swimming in cream, Tansy said, "Oh, he doesn't know." And hopefully, for everyone's sake, he never would. As completely as she believed the words, her heart told her they weren't true. She'd fallen in love with him.

"Then why is he here?" Clarice asked.

Hiding her feelings, Tansy answered, "Because he's a nice man. He has a daughter, Gracie Jane, whom I tutored while I was there." Thoughts of the six-year-old made her eyes well with tears, which also clogged her throat. "We became very close, so I can only assume that he needs to know I'm safe so Gracie Jane won't worry."

"But couldn't the two of you work out something?" Sally asked.

Tansy finished her breakfast, poured herself another cup of tea, and began the saga of Jesse's experience with both the Jarvis Mines, and an ex-socialite wife. Both women sat rapt, barely breathing as Tansy's story unfolded.

When she'd finished, Clarice sat there quiet. Sally, however, was in a state of despair. "You mean that just because he had a wife who came from money and who disappointed him and his daughter, he thinks all such women are like that?"

"Before he knew who I was, he had absolutely nothing good to say about any of us."

Clarice spoke up. "But that's like saying if one apple in the basket is bad, all of the rest of them must be as well."

"And dear sister, someone who worked at the mine allowed his cousin to die. But it wasn't Papa. Surely Mr. Wolfe can't blame us for that. I would bet you that if it had happened when Papa was there things would have turned out differently."

Yes, Tansy had often wondered about that…

"When do you expect your baby's birth?" Sally asked.

Tansy thought a moment. "I'm not sure. Perhaps in May?"

"He should be told," Clarice said, almost under her breath

then immediately apologized. "It's not my place to say anything. I'm sorry."

"No. I suppose you're right, but I don't want any sympathy from anyone. I went into this knowing full well what might happen. At the time, when I thought I was married, it didn't matter a whit because I wanted it."

Sally tsked, blushing. "Really, Anastasia, you talk so freely…"

"Yes, I know. And it's so emancipating. I enjoyed every minute we spent together."

Her sister's blush was obvious. "But…what will you do after, you know, the baby arrives?"

Sally's question was a good one. And one Tansy hadn't thought too hard on to this point. "I don't know. But I do know one thing. I am not giving it up."

Both Sally and Clarice gasped.

"Oh, god," Sally whispered. "Mama will have a stroke."

Tansy's anger peaked. "Mama? Where is she anyway? According to Oliver, she was as complicit as he was in determining that I wasn't sane. But then again, he could always convince her of whatever it was he was thinking."

Sally and Clarice exchanged glances. "She's at home. Oh, Anastasia, you know how she is. She's so certain that everyone is judging the family poorly because of what you did—"

"And what of Oliver? What does she think of him now? She told me once that if I'd only do what he says, I wouldn't get slapped." She was angry with her mother. Did she feel differently now, knowing what a flim-flam artist Oliver was?

"She's not strong like you are," Sally explained.

"What am I to do? Go and apologize to her for escaping an abusive marriage because the neighbors are talking behind her back?"

"That's her world," Sally offered.

"Yes, I know. And it was never mine," Tansy said. "Well, I don't have to stay in Chicago after the baby is born. Heaven forbid I give the neighborhood something else to talk about."

"But where will you go?" Sally's face was pale.

Tansy studied her pretty sister and then gave her a perky

smile. "Maybe I'll move to Atlanta. Would you disown me as well?"

"I couldn't possibly. Your nieces would have *me* sent away if they couldn't coddle and pamper a new cousin." She shook her head. "I'm just sorry your sheriff won't be part of the picture."

Tansy could have told her how Jesse's attitude toward her changed once he learned who she was. To be honest, the word 'love' never came up between them, although she knew in her heart that this man could be her world, if she could convince him to come into it.

Exhausted, Tansy didn't protest when Clarice led her toward the bedroom. "I'll be fine in a few minutes," she promised. Three hours later she was still sound asleep.

CHAPTER 26

*O*nce she woke and everyone sat in the sitting room again, Jacob joined them. Tansy didn't ask about Jesse, but she wasn't disappointed when he didn't show up. She still didn't feel strong enough to face him. Clarice stood behind her, fluffing her newly washed curls and gently messaging her scalp and shoulders. All of these wonderful things that had happened to her so quickly…Tansy couldn't believe a person could go from hell to heaven in mere hours, but she was here to say they could.

Tansy had learned only the bare bones of Oliver's deception on their way to the hotel, but now Jacob began to relate the full details. "Oliver grew up in the London slums. At an early age he learned that to survive. He had to cheat, lie, and steal. His mother was an alcoholic, and he never knew his father. Oliver was fifteen when there was an investigation into his mother's death. The law suspected Oliver had something to do with it, but they could never prove it. As he got older and his skills honed, he realized that by impersonating someone else and shedding his own poverty-ridden background, he could get what he wanted. And he wanted what every affluent man had."

Tansy sat, rapt. "So, he wasn't Oliver Radcliffe at all? Ever?" All of this news made her dizzy, so much information coming at her so fast. "And he may have killed his own mother?"

"Even at fifteen he was a clever lad, so I'm told. And his real name is Jasper Jaye."

Tansy repeated the name. She was numb. "Where is he now?"

Jacob answered, "We contacted Scotland Yard, and they verified that he is still wanted in London for theft, forgery, and public brawling during which time a Bobby was killed. Oliver *is* guilty of that death."

Still amazed, she asked, "So he's been arrested?"

"And he's being transported back to London as we speak, Anastasia."

Sally cleared her throat. "And apparently you weren't the first heiress he married. Unfortunately for that one, she put so much faith in his charm and 'knowledge' about her finances that she gave him her fortune to invest further. Needless to say, he invested it in himself and left her nearly penniless."

Tansy sat, dumfounded. "So, the private school, the diplomas, the degrees, the masses of kudos he received for work he'd claimed to have done...it was all a sham."

When Jacob nodded, Tansy asked, "How did you find out about this?"

Sally took her hand. "Mamie found a letter in one of your books written to you from Papa, explaining everything, how he'd discovered Oliver's true identity and all the sordid details. But then he died, and the book was never opened again until now."

"*Little Women.* The morning after he passed, I went into his den and picked up the book, but I couldn't bear to open it." How she regretted that decision now! Or did she? Everything that had transpired since her escape was something she would never forget. Something squeezed her heart, and she took a quick breath. At the same time her baby gave her a nice, firm kick.

"Now," Sally began. "Whether you want to see Jesse or not, he wants to see you before he leaves for California."

Tansy leaned back against the sofa and closed her eyes. "California. Maybe one day I'll get back there." She saw the ocean in her mind's eye and could almost smell the spray, see the whales, and hear the screams of the seagulls. "You know, I'd always rather thought that seagulls were pretty white birds, but

Jesse informed me that they are actually considered 'rats of the ocean.' I guess they're really filthy.

"But what Papa said about California is true. The ocean, the mountains, the smell of heat as it comes off the pine needles," she recalled with a smile. "The first time I smelled it I suggested we bottle it and sell it." A warm peace came over her when she thought about that visit. "Jesse's aunts live in a cabin near a river. I was only there once, but I remember every moment. I've tucked the memories away in my heart. Oh, I know that sounds silly, but...I really miss it."

No one interrupted her, so she went on, still envisioning the scene. "We had fresh fish for supper. And think how I must have looked, wearing one of the aunt's clothing, so I could provide the fish myself! I didn't care. It was all heavenly. You can hear the river burbling over the rocks, and even though it gets warm during the day, fog comes in off the ocean and cools everything off at night. And then it's gone by noon. It's unbelievable. I wouldn't have supposed such a place existed if I hadn't seen it myself." She sighed again and rubbed her stomach. "It would be a wonderful place to raise a child."

"What!"

Tansy's eyes popped open. The room was empty save for Jesse, who stood looking down at her, his expression both angry and bewildered.

"Jesse! How long have you been standing there?" She scooted farther down the sofa to create space between them.

"Long enough," he said gruffly.

Tansy allowed her gaze to wander slowly over his body. He was so tall, her face fit into the well of his neck, and she loved his smell. "Well, I will miss California," she said stubbornly. Tears stung. "And I will miss Gracie Jane and Ruta and Will and Walt and Zeb..." She hiccoughed a sob. "And...and I would miss you, Jesse, if I never saw you again. I would miss everything. Oh, I hate to cry. Don't make me cry, Jesse, I'm ugly when I cry."

He bit back a smile. "Who told you that?"

She could have told him, but it wasn't important. Mama always said ladies don't cry in public. Oliver, the snake, told her that when she cried, she looked like a big, sad clown. "It doesn't matter now."

He sat down beside her, reached out, but drew his hand back. "You're pregnant."

She gave him a puzzled look. "Yes. I am. And I've been through hell, Jesse, especially when I realized I could lose the baby in the asylum. And, for your information, I could probably live without you, but I don't want to. Jesse, I love you, and I can't stand the thought of you not seeing our baby."

Jesse growled and turned away. "Don't." He ran his fingers through his hair, stood and began to pace. "You have everything. What could I give you that you don't already have?"

She pressed her hand to her abdomen. "You've already given me something I've never had."

He still didn't appear convinced. He rubbed the back of his neck and shook his head. "How can you possibly be happy with me after living the way you have?"

"I was never as happy as I've been with you and Gracie Jane. Don't be fooled, Jesse. Money and privilege don't necessarily mean happiness. I want more than anything to be with you and Gracie Jane. I want this baby to have a sister and a mother and a father who love it. I want to live near the ocean so that each day I can walk the beach with my children in tow, play in the surf, collect seashells, and watch for whales.

"I want to fish in Little Sur. I want to build us a place near your aunts, so that they can be a part of our lives. I want to climb to your tree house and look out over the vastness of the ocean. Maybe even sleep up there one night, high in the trees with you by my side. I want to smell the pine needles. I want a place that I have chosen to raise our family."

He was quiet for so long, she became afraid, for all she'd been talking about was herself.

"You're saying you don't want to live at the boarding house?"

She pressed her hands over her mouth to stop a smile. "If that's what it takes for us to be together, I'll even consider that."

He sat beside her again and took her hand. His was huge, warm, and calloused. She remembered the first time she noticed how different it was from Oliver's. "I still don't know how you can leave all this and come with me."

"Don't you want me to?" she asked it lightly.

He drew her close and pressed his hand against what was left of her hair. "More than you'll ever know."

EPILOGUE

By the Little Sur River

*I*nsects hummed in the dry, warm air. The breeze was soft. It rustled her curls, which she opted to keep short after her month in hell four years ago. She and Jesse had married soon after she left the asylum. And not long after that, she had a little girl they named Caroline, after Jesse's mother.

And now she had another baby, a son they named Jonah Ernest, after Jesse's cousin and Tansy's father. He was barely a year and walked early, perhaps eager to get on with his young life. Both of their children, Jonah and Caroline, who was three, had Tansy's dark curls. She gazed at the hanging flower baskets Em had put up on the porch of her and Jesse's new home. The smell was intoxicating.

By cabin standards, the house was large. It had a great room with a fireplace that separated it from a large kitchen. Tansy had insisted the kitchen be big enough for them to eat in. She still loved the kitchen, even though she wasn't a cook. Em and May took turns doing that. She had learned to bake, however, and her ginger cookies were excellent. Everyone said so. There were four bedrooms, all comfortable and roomy. And the most precious part of the house for Tansy was the crow's nest, a small room up three flights of winding stairs where she could look out over the ocean. It was her private place, although she shared it with everyone.

Gracie Jane waved at her from the grass, where she was trying to teach Caroline to toss a ball. She kept handing 'Sissy,' as they called her, the ball in her right hand, and Caroline insisted on using her left.

"She won't use the proper hand," Gracie Jane complained. Gracie Jane's arthritis had been in remission for three years. She was lively, could run and play with others, but still preferred to read and play the piano. She devoured books greedily. Jesse built a bookcase in her room, which she added to every chance she got.

Tansy shaded her eyes with her hand. "Let her use the one she wants, honey."

Clarice stepped out onto the porch. "Jonah is still napping. Are you ready for some tea?" Before leaving Chicago, Tansy had convinced Clarice to accompany her to California. She would be a wonderful companion for Gracie Jane. It had worked out well. They adored one another. And interestingly, Lloyd, who was the new sheriff in town, had come calling not long after they all settled in. Tansy expected she would lose Clarice very soon. A wedding was in the cards.

"Tea sounds wonderful. Is there still some of that delicious cake Em brought over yesterday?" Amazingly, since her pregnancies, Tansy could eat whatever she wanted and had slimmed down in spite of it.

"I'll get it," Clarice answered.

The boarding house was still up and running, Ruta at the helm, but Margot, younger and stronger, did more than her share of the work. And to everyone's surprise, Ellis Crawford, the private investigator who was hired to find Tansy, had showed up on the porch one day, asking for a room. That was two years ago. He was still there, and it seemed he had his sights set on Margot. They discovered he was a pretty fair handyman, and he had the funds to fix what was needed to keep everyone inside warm and dry.

Also, before she left Chicago, Tansy learned that the woman she'd met at the asylum, Mary Clara Brooks, had become newly widowed, and her grown son petitioned to have her released. True to her word, Mrs. Brooks began to write about the conditions in the asylum. With Tansy's help, she found a newspaper man who agreed to publish the pieces monthly in his paper, *The Penny Press*. Tansy continued to support the project with enthusiasm.

Lloyd became something of a hero in Willow River when he caught his brother, Lester, and his cronies, clubbing sea otters to death and selling their pelts to a company in the south. Of course, Jesse had started the investigation, but he was happy to let Lloyd have all the credit.

With Jesse's knowledge of the forest, birds, and animals and his awareness of the need to safeguard particular sea and land creatures, the newly established Forest Service hired him. Sometimes he was gone for days at a time, but Tansy knew he was finally a happy man. They didn't speak of her money, and of course, she had to threaten Jesse with an iron skillet if he didn't allow them to have the house she wanted built with it. Not that she would ever have used it. Physical and mental abuses were not things they worried about in their marriage.

At that moment he came through the trees and strode to her, waving the mail. He was still so handsome, so tall, so... unbelievably sensual. She would not have believed she could love him more as the years went by. The pulse at her throat throbbed at the sight of him. And even after four years of marriage, the looks between them were private and electric.

He bent down and kissed her. "Met the mail wagon on the road." He handed her a letter and a newspaper and ducked as Pesky soared in, dropping a big pinecone on the porch. The bird came around often, although he didn't always leave a gift.

Tansy took the mail from Jesse. "The letter is from Sally," she said, eager to read it.

"What does it say?" Gracie Jane had run to the porch.

"Yeth," Caroline lisped, "what doth it thay?" She always copied her sister. She adored her.

They were trying to teach her not to lisp, but she was only three. They had time.

Tansy scanned the letter. "Sally says that despite her own reluctance and Mama's insistence, Mamie will have a debutante ball in Atlanta in the spring."

Gracie Jane clasped her hands to her chest. "Oh, a ball! Could we go, Mama?"

It hadn't taken her long to refer to Tansy as her mother. No one had coaxed her. It was what she wanted to do.

"That would be exciting, wouldn't it?" She turned to Jesse. "I know it's a long way off, but can we try to make the trip?" Money wasn't the issue of course, but Jesse was well-respected among the Forest Service personnel and often called away unexpectedly.

He squeezed her shoulder. "I'd love to see Sally and Jacob and the girls. Your mother, well, that's another story," he added, so only she could hear it. "I'll get you more tea."

She mouthed 'thank you' and watched him disappear into the cabin.

Grace Jarvis had not changed. She viewed Tansy's marriage as far beneath her station. Although she was generous with her new grandchildren, she rarely had much time for Jesse. Or Tansy, for that matter. Tansy had come to terms with that. No matter what went on in her life, things would never change between Grace Jarvis and her youngest daughter, and because Tansy was so deliriously happy, she had come to settle for that.

Tansy put the letter aside and opened the paper. In this issue of *The Penny Press* was another segment of Mary Clara's essay on the conditions of the asylum.

Dear Readers,

Who are the subjects of insane asylums? They are of any class or stature. They are married women with children to care for whose husbands have deemed them unfit, for any number of reasons. Your past, your financial records, or social relations are not important. You have no rights. You are legally dead. You will have a trial, but it is a hoax, for whoever has consigned you to this hell has all the ammunition he or she needs to put you there. Perhaps you complained about the way your husband spent money. One day, you return from church to find a housekeeper living in your home. Furious, you take some of your own clothing off the line, and the next thing you know you are accused of theft and insanity and sent away, your children scattered to the winds. What a convenient way to get rid of you! Perhaps your personal life is fraught with illness. You are useless to a husband who is eager to start anew with someone else. You languish in a hovel of hell where you somehow survive in a room with ten other women, some truly insane, some as sane as you are. But beware! Should you complain of these conditions, you will be relegated to an even worse fate!

I have seen dead bodies carried over an assistant's shoulder like a side of beef to be either discarded or sold, perhaps to a hospital for medical students to practice upon…or worse. I have witnessed women unable to care for themselves being put in a hot bath, their heads held under water until they fainted. I bear witness to the fact that the staff dines like royalty, while the patients eat the dregs. I have seen women who have undergone procedures that have left them simple, unable to converse or interact or be as they were before all in the name of a medical cure. Shock therapy? It exists. Insulin therapy? It exists.

Next time I shall share more details of the deplorable conditions of insane asylums with you. I write these words confidently as I lived them and am fortunate to be here to share them with you.

Mary Clara Brooks

Tansy folded the paper and put it beside her chair. She didn't always want to read things that took her back to the hell she'd been in. But she knew it was important to keep the public informed as to what transpired behind those awful closed doors.

She glanced up and focused on her children. They brought her such unbelievable joy that she often wondered how she'd become such a lucky woman. Fate steps in, doesn't it?

Without her unhappiness with Oliver, she never would have escaped. Without her father's love of Willow River, she would never have found Jesse. And Gracie Jane. And the wonderful love they all shared.

She caught Jesse's eye as he returned to the porch with her cup of tea. In his eyes, she saw his love for her. And that was all she ever wanted.

Don't miss out on your next favorite book!

Join the Satin Romance mailing list
www.satinromance.com/mail.html

THANK YOU FOR READING

Did you enjoy this book?

We invite you to leave a review at your favorite book site, such as Goodreads, Amazon, Barnes & Noble, etc.

DID YOU KNOW THAT LEAVING A REVIEW...

- Helps other readers find books they may enjoy.
- Gives you a chance to let your voice be heard.
- Gives authors recognition for their hard work.
- Doesn't have to be long. A sentence or two about why you liked the book will do.

ABOUT THE AUTHOR

Jane's first historical romance, *Secrets of a Midnight Moon*, was heralded as 'sensitive and sensuous, violent and tender.'

"I found the plot to my first novel in a little known history of Northern California Indians when I learned that Native Americans were being taken as slaves by the settlers, their families threatened with death and dismemberment if they tried to leave. Yes, one can weave a romance around such an appalling event!"

"I found the plot to my first novel in a little known history of Northern California Indians when I learned that Native Americans were being taken as slaves by the settlers, their families threatened with death and dismemberment if they tried to leave. Yes, one can weave a romance around such an appalling event!"

Since then she has published nine full length novels and four anthologies, all dealing with the perils and passions of romantic historical fiction.

She graduated from the University of Minnesota majoring in American and Russian History revealing that, "while all of my stories are set in the US, I had hoped one day to set one in Russia, though in my opinion, the best ones have already been written."

Jane continues to write and also edits for Melange Books. She currently lives in St. Paul, Minnesota with her husband, Richard Noer.

f facebook.com/janejbonander

BB bookbub.com/authors/jane-bonander